About the Author

Benjamin Kwakye was born in Accra, Ghana and attended the Presbyterian Secondary School in Ghana, and Dartmouth College and Harvard Law School in the US. At Dartmouth, he majored in Government (with an emphasis in international relations), spending trimesters in Arles, France and the London School of Economics (LSE) and the United Nations Association in New York. He wrote and published poetry while in college, served as editor of *Spirit* (a literary journal of Dartmouth College's African American Society) and received the Society's 1990 Senior Honor Roll for outstanding leadership, distinguished service and intellectual and artistic creativity. His first novel, *The Clothes of Nakedness* (1998) won the 1999 Commonwealth Writers' Prize for Best First Book (Africa Region) and has been adapted for radio as a BBC *Play of the Week*. His second novel *The Sun by Night* (2005) won the 2006 Commonwealth Writers Prize for Best Book (Africa Section). He is a director of The Africa Education Initiative, a non-profit organization dedicated to promoting science education in Africa. He lives near Chicago.

About the Book

The Other Crucifix marks its narratorial brilliance magisterially with themes hitherto only minimally expressed and unexplored at length in African and African American fiction. In a brilliantly crafted tale of student activism, blissful and delicately sweet-turned-sour companionship and marriage with Fiona, followed by vagrancy and testing fatherhood that directly relates some very rich African American experiences with an immigrant African's story of struggle and survival in the United States. Lead protagonist Ghanaian Jojo Badu gives us insights not only into the most intimate and intricate details of the lives of his several interesting characters, but connects his highly interiorised personal narrative with the politics of other stories of global solidarity. In this sense, while Benjamin Kwakye's highly stimulating and engaging narrative is a novel of epic proportions, reminiscent of such classics within the African literary canon as Syl Cheney Coker's *The Last Harmattan of Alusine Dunbar*, Ben Okri's The Famished Road and lately Ngugi wa Thiongo's *Wizard of the Crow*, it stamps its own revelatory and reflective authority on contemporary African fiction.

Kwadwo Osei-Nyame, Jnr
Lecturer in African Literature
Culture and Diasporan Studies
SOAS, University of London

BENJAMIN KWAKYE

The Other Crucifix

A NOVEL

An Adinkra symbol meaning
Ntesie maternasie
A symbol of knowledge and wisdom

First published in the UK by Ayebia Clarke Publishing Limited in 2010
7 Syringa Walk
Banbury
Oxfordshire
OX16 1FR
UK
www.ayebia.co.uk

ISBN 978-0-9562401-2-5

Distributed outside Africa, Europe and the United Kingdom
and exclusively in the US by
Lynne Rienner Publishers Inc
1800 30th Street, Suite 314
Boulder, CO 80301
USA
www.rienner.com

Distributed in the UK and Europe by TURNAROUND Publishing Services
at Wood Green, London, UK www.turnaround-uk.com

Distributed in Southern Africa by Book Promotions a subsidiary of Jonathan Ball
Publishers in South Africa. For orders contact: orders@bookpro.co.za

Co-published and distributed in Ghana with the Centre for Intellectual Renewal
56 Ringway Estate, Osu, Accra, Ghana.

British Library Cataloguing-in-Publication Data
Cover Design by Amanda Carroll at Millipedia, UK.
Cover images from Getty Images.
Typeset by FiSH Books, Enfield, Middlesex, UK.

Available from www.ayebia.co.uk or email info@ayebia.co.uk
Distributed in Africa, Europe, UK by TURNAROUND at www.turnaround-uk.com

The Publisher wishes to acknowledge the support of Arts Council SE Funding

To Esi, with love
We always keep the gold

Acknowledgements

I am deeply grateful to my family members for the support they continue to provide me and for creating a loving environment for my creative endeavors, even when they render me incommunicado for long periods. To my friends who continue to nourish me with words of support, I say thank you for not deserting me when numerous phone calls remain unreturned. To my colleagues at work, thanks for allowing me to balance the challenges of a fulltime job with the demands of writing. To my Oasis family, thanks for your prayers. I am also deeply indebted to Nana Ayebia Clarke for her tireless efforts and support in bringing this book to fruition. God bless you, one and all.

One

Was my arrival in the US a day to curse or bless? I have to step back a little to rescue that memory from increasing obscurity and the blitz of my successes and failures, hopes and regrets. The journey from Boston Logan Airport had been by bus; before that, a seven-hour journey by plane from Accra to Zurich, where I remained in transit for six hours, before emplaning for the US. I remembered my brothers, sisters and parents at the airport, beaming with farewells, as dusk deepened into darkness, reminding me to stay in touch often. God be with you, they said in continual chorus. I regretted that Marjorie had refused to come to the airport. She couldn't bear it, she said, having wept uncontrollably the night before.

Thoughts of home would nag me. Years after my arrival, questions would abide, casting a long spectre of doubt. What if I'd stayed in Ghana, land of my birth, embodiment of my past? What if I had gone to Ghana Law School, married a Ghanaian woman, bred children who spoke Asante and swam in the same waters as I, recognised the same landmarks as I did and my forebears before me? What if I'd established my practice there; aged without the sense of abandonment rattling as chains on my heels and canvassed perhaps for a political office or two? *The Road Not Taken*, I do not remember thee with just a sigh, as though you were a potential simply submerged in the success of *The Road Taken*. But even success is a loaded word, for I have beaten my chest like a madman and yelled at the forgone possibilities, held between the reality of today and the receding, unreachable, past. I have yelled like a lunatic at the inconclusiveness of my choices. In a way, the road not taken became a dream that never was, a suspension of tomorrow that, because of its lack of fulfillment, came with considerable regret. Perhaps that isn't bad after all – a life without regret implies a perfect life or one without ambition, lived too glibly, without trial and growth. But, at the same time, a life filled with regret is a sad one, even depressing, perhaps. Or is regret merely an offshoot of satisfaction, feeding off it and vice versa?

"You'll meet another woman and forget about me," she said. My Marjorie. How could I ever leave her? "I love your deep, loud voice," she said after watching me in a debate in secondary school. "It takes control of the room." I'd seen her before, but for the first time I noticed the woman behind the girl: generosity in size of nose, lips, bosom and behind; even her eyes were large, the skin so pitch black she stood out among dark skinned people. She kept her hair natural and closely cropped and wore little makeup. A natural beauty. I fell in love with her at first voice – when I heard her speak for the first time. "I promise you I'll never leave you." A promise made to be upheld or broken?

To be broken, she must have prophesied silently. To be upheld, I believed. I knew her expressions too well, the wistfulness that betrayed doubts. I had none. What could I do to prove my commitment? I was surprised by the thought that I seized upon. It was daring, maybe even stupid. I had heard or perhaps read about it somewhere and dismissed it as sentimental foolishness. But once I thought of it, I felt compelled to express it in deed. It seemed as adventurous as it seemed a bold statement of my love. To me, this must have been the way a novelist writes a worthy epic: with pain, daring and foolishness. For me, what words couldn't accomplish, blood would put together. And what blood has put together let no one dare put asunder. To me, I was writing the epic of our love – boldly, brashly and daringly. I picked up a razor blade. She pulled away, concerned. "Trust me," I said. I made a small cut in the middle of my thumb. She gasped. I took her thumb and as she looked away, I cut her the same way. She flinched. Then I put the two thumbs together and rubbed them hard. "By this act, I commit to you," I said. "This is my promise to you." Rituals of love, like rituals of death. Meaningful. Meaningless. Marjorie wept. And whether the epic would end with this act or renew itself with new meanings and last through time remained to be determined. Afraid she couldn't keep composed, she'd opted not to share a last farewell at the airport. But what could be more meaningful than our exchange of blood? This was the woman I loved. This was the woman I'd marry. No high tide could flood my love, I affirmed; and no low tide could strand it. "Stay the good course," I said over and again.

I was inflated with anxiety and excitement, this being my first trip ever out of Ghana. I dreamed of opportunity and hope, but I feared the unknown. Amid the apprehension and Marjorie's tearful absence, however, I found some solace in my family, whose presence fortified me a little for the journey.

I'd never sat in a plane. I'd heard others say it's like being in a bus, only you're suspended in space. Wide eyed when I first entered, I braced myself for long moments of horrifying flight time. But I played the part of the confident globetrotter. And in my three-piece suit I thought I looked the part. There were a few comic errors, I suppose: not knowing how to buckle the seat belt or handle the armrest controls (and each time watching the man next to me before I did anything) or not knowing what food to order and saying yes when asked if I wanted chicken or pasta (forcing the flight attendant to repeat the question and having the man next to me pick chicken on my behalf) or being a bit confused in the restroom by which button controlled what function. Even worse were the six hours in transit I spent at Zurich airport – hungry and reaching a cafeteria and not recognizing the foods. I left without ordering, choosing hunger over embarrassment. The airport seemed so big I didn't know where to go to connect to the next flight. After repeated attempts in very slow English, I managed to communicate my problem to an airport official who directed me, in English I found difficult to understand, to the appropriate gate. It'd get better, I said. These are not native English speakers. Once I arrive in America, native speakers will understand me and I them.

Two

My memory of Logan, another massive airport, is misty, and worsened by the anxiety and confusion I recall feeling at the time. I was seeking familiarity in an unfamiliar place. I remembered the immigration official checking my papers. "Are you going back home or are you going to be like those who stay here after they're done with school?" I was offended by her presumptuousness. How dare she ask me that? Did she not know of Marjorie waiting? Did she not know that Uncle Kusi had hopes for me? But frozen somewhat by the badge of her authority, I said nothing. And years later as I remained in America I would be shamed to remember that question, knowing that I had confirmed her suspicion.

My goal at the time was to return home and work with Uncle Kusi. He wasn't an uncle by blood or marriage, just a man my father had done some work for who seemed to like me and had become a family friend. Childless, he often introduced me to his friends as his nephew. He said I was intelligent and would go far if I had the appropriate opportunities. He'd earned a bachelor's degree, but wasn't interested in the tedium of office work. Instead, with inherited money, he'd started as a timber merchant and later initiated a myriad of businesses. He was everywhere, collected and drove luxury cars, dated beautiful women and was mentioned as a potential leader in government. He was so powerful he had enormous influence in the ruling party at the time.

Before I left, he'd told me, "Don't stay too long in America. They will turn you into a eunuch. Come back home. I'll find a place for you in my business. Someday, you and I can rule this country, Jojo. You have the intelligence. And that booming voice of yours is just perfect for politics." I was so proud of him. I loved him deeply. Too bad that Papa wasn't like Uncle Kusi, Uncle Kusi who taught me chess. Not that I played it well or frequently. "This is one of the best games you'll ever learn," he said, spreading the chessboard carefully in front of him as though it was his most valuable possession, this man who possessed mansions, and held men's esteem and women's affections. "Your goal is simple," he said. "You want to checkmate your opponent's king; that is, so the king can't make another move without being captured." Uncle Kusi arranged the chess pieces on the board. "Sounds simple, doesn't it? But it's not. It requires wit, patience and awareness, an awareness that takes your opponent's weaknesses into account and exploits them. If you don't, he will exploit yours. Always remember that. You must not assume otherwise. But the problem is that you may not know how to identify such weaknesses, unless you've played your opponent before. So what if you haven't? Then you must rely on your knowledge, intelligence and focus. It's important for the beginner to take lessons from those who've played it before. In fact, for the beginner, this could be a sort of advantage. You see, it's like the concept of *Sankofa* ... reaching back and taking from the wealth of history." Uncle Kusi winked, but he spoke so seriously I knew he was asking for my attention. Undivided. "One other thing is to start with your endgame. Begin at the end?

Yes, that's exactly what you need to do and you'll be way ahead of your opponent. Better to know where you intend to end. You can hardly go wrong if you combine that and the knowledge you acquire from those who've played it before and your own experience. Even if you don't win, you'd play the game better." I stored his advice somewhere in those deep fissures of memory that are never consulted until occasion necessitates.

After sidling around the immigration official's question, I claimed my luggage and moved to Customs, where my bags were scrupulously searched. The official stared at me and asked matter-of-factly, "Where are you going, nigger?" He spoke so calmly, as if bidding me welcome. Maybe he *was* bidding me welcome. But at the time, the question was as meaningless to me as any. It seemed expressed without offense. I ignored it, for what did *nigger* really mean to me when stripped of its dispiriting cultural and historical contexts? Not that I was devoid of race consciousness. I had read about America and its conflicts, about the struggles of its black sons and daughters. So sure, I knew the word had negative connotations, but it is one thing to read and another to live and experience it. Without the context that gives words bone and flesh and form, without the torrid undercurrent that gives certain words meaning, it seemed like a bad joke rather than a malignant query. If I were asked that question years later, I would fully experience its flesh, its bones, its venoms and I would have my arms ready to counter. And years later, I would wonder if he had known how green I was. With his training and experience, had he guessed I'd just arrived from Africa? Welcome to America, he might as well have said.

After I cleared Customs, I asked and received directions to the Greyhound bus station. Getting there required another short bus ride. I soon realised that the English spoken here wasn't my English. Accent aside, the quickness with which words were spoken and the slang that dotted expressions required patient decoding, and I sometimes had to appreciate the gist of speech rather than understand everything. As for my English, I had to repeat myself several times. Sometimes, my listeners would rephrase my words as questions to clarify my meaning and *correct* my pronunciations.

The hustle and shuffle all around confused me, but I was in America and was sustained by my sense of arrival, that I'd achieved something worthwhile – and was in a land famed for freedom, opportunity, democracy and justice. I had read the Declaration of Independence over and again and relished its "self-evident truths": of all being born equal with inalienable rights that included life, liberty and the pursuit of happiness. Here's where I'd earn my education, work no more than two years for practical training and return to help the country of my birth. Marjorie was waiting. Uncle Kusi was waiting. Ghana was waiting. I figured America had a lot to offer me. Hadn't both countries withstood British rule and survived? Ghana, as I saw it, was in a way like America at independence: bold, idealistic and unstoppable. I pondered these matters as I boarded the bus, then slept most of the journey. I was still exhausted, though, when I arrived on campus.

With two suitcases in hand, I went in search of my dorm room. I found it bare with two desks and chairs in the living room and two twin sized beds in the bedroom. Nothing more. It had a strange emptiness and artificiality to it. Somehow, it seemed to emit unpleasant memories. It wasn't just uninhabited, it seemed uninhabitable. And I was alone. For the first time, I knew it. Going away to boarding school a mere thirty minutes from home aged twelve had not affected me like this. There's no comparison in being among strangers who shared the same language or culture or country and being miles away from home among . . . what? I would find out.

I shoved both suitcases inside the bedroom closet and fell on one undressed mattress to sleep, trapped as I was by physical and emotional exhaustion. I woke up later to sounds from the living room, voices that spoke boisterously and seemingly with familiarity to one another. Familiarity. Where was mine? I had to purge my mind to escape the threat of nostalgia. I could ill afford such self-pitying sentiments if I were to thrive. *Marjorie, where are you?*

I would soon meet my first American family, but I hesitated. What did I have to say to them? How should I introduce myself? Through the bedroom window, I saw it was darkening outside. Either way I would have to act, by going into the living room or continuing to feign sleep. But I knew that to be introduced to America, I had to start somewhere. Slowly I opened the door to the living room, and was immediately shocked by the transformation. How long had I slept? There was a couch in the centre of the room sitting over an oriental carpet. A television was mounted in one corner and in the other corner a radio played the Chiffon's 'He's Fine' in low volume. A poster of two scantily clad women adorned one wall of the room.

"Hi." A tall, silver haired man walked over to me, offered a hand and said, "My name's Mark Palmer. This is my wife Anne and this here is my son Ed."

His handshake was the firmest I'd ever experienced

(and I'd soon learn that it was the American way). My tentative shake must have seemed wimpy to him. I shook the equally svelte Anne Palmer's hand and then Ed's. "My name is Jojo Badu."

So these were the Palmers. The Residence Office had sent me a note two months earlier notifying me of my roommate: Edward Palmer, Somerville, Massachusetts. And here he was, pleasant, smiling. His long, almost unkempt hair fell to his shoulders, abundant as his moustache and the beard that must have been an inch long. It seemed his attempts to grow full sideburns had failed so that only stubs lined the sides of his face. Ed appeared not to belong to his parents: meticulous grooming on the part of the elders against something approaching slovenliness on the part of the offspring. Opposites beget opposites? I smiled back. The Palmers were strangers, even if strangers in close environs; but in the knowledge that Ed Palmer would be my roommate for the next year, I was already forcing a bridge over the valley that separates strangers.

"We thought we ought not to bug you," Mark Palmer explained, "You were sleeping when we got in."

"You must be exhausted, coming all the way from Ghana," Anne said.

"The journey was very tiring."

"How long did it take?" asked Ed.

"The whole journey took twenty-one hours if you include transit time."

"And we thought it was a hassle driving two hours from Somerville," Mark said.

"It must be awful . . . you know, coming all this way, coming so far from home," Anne remarked.

"Well . . ."

"Do you have any family in the States?" she asked.

"I've heard there's a distant relative somewhere."

"Where at?"

"Chicago."

"That must be so hard. Being stuck in New Hampshire."

"Oh Mom, he'll manage," said Ed.

I understood most of what they said, occasionally having to guess when they spoke too fast. I learned (a little later) that Mark Palmer was an ophthalmologist; Anne a real estate agent. Ed was an only child. "We've spoilt him," Anne said, "so be careful."

"Well, Jojo," Mark Palmer said, "We didn't have to travel across seas so we brought a lot of stuff with us. I hope they don't get in the way. We've got to get going, so you guys be good." He again offered his hand to me and said, "It was nice meeting you."

Anne Palmer did the same, adding, "If you guys need anything, just call."

After they'd left, Ed asked, "You're hungry? I'm starving."

"Yes, I haven't eaten in a while."

"Come on then, let's get a bite."

"A what?"

"Let's get something to eat."

"Do you know where we're going?" I asked.

"Sure, I took a tour of campus. I'm sure I remember where the cafeteria's at."

We walked across the centre of campus. The library rose on our right as its clock chimed six times. We went past administrative buildings and entered the cafeteria. Immediately, I was impressed by the array of food available and the seemingly endless choice of drinks, desserts and fruits. I took a moment to ponder and then I gazed at the servers in the serving line.

"What can I get you, honey?" one of them asked.

I didn't recognise the food. I didn't know what to say. "I have not decided yet," I said. "Go ahead and get what you want," I suggested to Ed. Then after Ed ordered, I followed him and said, "I will have the same thing."

It was only after I'd sat down to eat that I studied what was on my tray. "What's that?" I asked.

"Clam chowder."

"And that?"

"Manicotti."

I struggled to finish the chowder. It was so bland.

"You don't like it?" Ed asked.

"The food I'm used to has a little more spice."

I couldn't finish the chowder, but the Manicotti was passable. I finished that. I watched Ed eat half of his plate and lose interest in the rest of the food. He didn't talk much, except to explore a little of my background. I was eager to ask him questions, this young man who would be my roommate for the year. Who was he? How would I find out? Where would I begin? Questions without answers; expectations without knowledge. Shouldn't we have come well catalogued and defined so we could find comfort in each other's company? Wasn't it too much to expect two strangers to live as roommates without such knowledge? *Who are you?* It was a question unasked, but one we both must have been asking silently and fully aware that, like a book, the answer couldn't be offered in one sentence or paragraph or chapter. This would have to be a painstaking study of the full text, a text without quick denouement, if ever it had one. That was the patience required. Did we have it? After our first supper, we stepped out together into the chilling dusk.

Three

The dusk seemed to yield too quickly to night. And in the night, before sleep came, I remembered the laughter of Papa bursting out like thunder, loud and uncontrolled. "My son, you have done well." That was laughter full of pride. "The University. You have done well indeed. Go and learn something and come back home and rule the country. You will do very well."

"I want to go to America too," Yaayaa was saying.

"Eat your food, Yaayaa," Mama said.

My sister shrugged and looked across at me – leaving soon for this famed land of greatness and plenty.

"We will come and visit you," my sister Ama said.

"I too will come to school there," said my brother Kofi.

"You'd better work harder in school, then," Papa advised. "How do you expect to get a scholarship with the kind of grades you're making?"

In my memory, I am looking at faces, Papa, Mama, Kofi, Yaayaa, Ama, Kwabena . . . and I am thinking how lucky I am. We are a poor family, eking out a living has been like running on an empty stomach with a headache too. It has been a strain on Mama and Papa, who are the breadwinners, but we (the children) also bear some of the burden. And now, with this partial scholarship, I have the opportunity to go to America and return with a degree from no less a school than The University, ranked among the top ten in the United States. I will return and become a leading member in society, serve the country in one capacity or the other. The year is 1963 and the country is beaming with optimism, still – six or so years after independence. I am thinking that I will become a leader. I could become Governor of the Bank of Ghana, managing director of some grand corporation. Who knows, I could even become president.

I had started on somewhat shaky ground in school. In primary school, my grades were just passable. But with a sprinter's focus, I had gained momentum in secondary school, challenged by Papa. "Do you want to disappoint me, Jojo?" he'd said. That was the first time the old man had questioned my scholarship. He'd watched (I know in dismay) as Kofi failed to register meaningful grades. And now I too was following that path. "Jojo, I hope you understand this. Your mother and I wake up early every-day to go to work to try and cater for you because we want a better life for you. You see how we suffer. I wasn't blessed with the opportunity you have. I had to start fending for myself at a very early age. Twelve and my father was dead. What could I do but start working to help my mother take care of my brothers and sisters? As the eldest in the family, I had no choice. And now, without an education, I am at the mercy of the powerful in society. I wish I had had the opportunity. Jojo, you have it now. Use it. Don't throw this away."

OK, Papa. He had challenged me. Would I meet the challenge? I was about twelve when he gave me that speech. Uncle Kusi rejoined, asking that I listen to Papa's advice. And so I tested myself and for the first time took my schoolwork seriously. No more winging it, throwing my chances away. I actually sat down and studied. And it began to show immediately. I couldn't be beaten in school, rising from nowhere to the top of my class. And once I got there, I never wavered. My academic record was, pardon me as I use the word, impeccable. From then on, my report card became unassailable: the grades were excellent, Jojo was "confident, possesses great leadership skills" (or variations of that theme). I was active in student government, eventually becoming head prefect. And when I addressed the school on Speech and Prize-Giving Day, I received a standing ovation and Marjorie fell in love with me. "You projected such confidence, such self-assuredness. You seemed poised to conquer the world. And your voice... what power it carries." Even Uncle Kusi remarked once, "With such a voice and character, you are destined to become a leader."

And when in my final year of secondary school I sauntered into the American Centre (more out of boredom than curiosity), my future was about to point in a different direction. I had been eyeing the University of Ghana all along and I was poised to go there. But as I sat in the visitors' lounge and read through pamphlets left there, I presume to present America in the best possible light, a woman walking by stopped, observed me for a minute and asked, "Do you like what you're reading?"

"It looks very interesting, America."

"It is."

"Do you miss it?"

"Yes, it's home. But I like being here, too."

"From what I know of it, it seems like a very vibrant country. Perhaps after I finish school and have some money I can visit it someday."

"You're in school?"

"Yes, final year of secondary school."

"Hmm. Have you thought about going to school in America?"

"Not seriously, I haven't."

"Maybe you should apply to a few schools and see what happens."

And I did. It happened that the lady, Tina Oliphant, was some sort of attaché at the US Centre. She offered me brochures about US colleges, pointing me to the good schools after I told her of my academic record. She would counsel me through the application process, encourage me when I lost interest...

Then I got the letter of admission to The University and I was headed for America, on a partial scholarship. More money would come from a work/study programme that allowed me to work on campus to pay for personal expenses and books, and the rest would be in loans.

Papa took me to the village to say farewell to grandfather. The old man pondered my departure for a long time. "Times have changed," he said, fidgeting with his shirt's buttons. "Why you should go to the white man's land to study shows that times have changed. I would rather you stayed at home, but that would be selfish of me. There's something, however, that I want you to remember. Do not stay too long in Amrika, you hear? You will never belong in the land of white people. The elders say that the foreigner never carries the head of the casket. Remember that. So finish your school and come back here where when you look around, it will be like looking in the mirror. In that land, you will never see your reflection when you look around. That is bad for the spirit. And that is all I have to say, my grandson. Go with God."

And within a week I was in America. But now that I was in America and seeking to discover it, I wanted to remember. I wanted to remember a December, any December, perhaps with the onset of the Harmattan season, which would normally bring dry cool winds from the north. I recalled hot and oppressive weather. But then I also recalled how quickly you get used to the Ghanaian heat. And because Accra sits on the Atlantic Ocean, its breeziness came to mind. I never wanted to forget what makes home *home*: family, the spiritual rebirth that comes with seeing familiar faces, seeing nephews and nieces, some of whom were little (and whom I may not see for a while) and the joy they would show on seeing me would reaffirm that home is where you go knowing that no matter what happens to you, no matter what others might think of you, you will be loved. Period. No ifs or buts. This is where the spirit feels most comfortable, most restful and most at ease.

I wanted never to forget – the beach on the Atlantic, where even the fishy smell of the ocean seems perfectly normal, where you can sit and watch the vast blue sea beat against the shore again and again and then see its reach into the vastness where it seems to touch the sky; on land, the coconut trees and the people who throng to the beach and dot the shore and a little father down the expensive, multi-starred hotels that are likely to be patronised by tourists or rich business people.

But why stop there? To really get a feel for Accra, I made my mind take a trip to any market where it's as if you have been transformed into a heaven of human activity – full of voices, shuffling feet and all assortments of food; traders, their foodstuffs arranged in their stalls, calling out to you to buy this or that: plantains, yams, cassava, fish, fruits, rice, clothes, necklaces; and mingling with the voices, the sounds of the cars passing by, honking or drivers yelling at pedestrians who seem to invade the streets. I recalled this massive cacophony that, like most things in Ghana, assumes friendliness and soon becomes familiar. If thirsty, I would sample (as I sampled in memory) some Ghanaian beer or, if I desired something sweeter but equally or more potent, I'd try some sweet palm wine or the sour millet drink called *pito*.

In my mind, I decided to check out many of the restaurants for some local food like fried plantains, rice and beans, *fufu* and *jolof* rice. In fact I didn't need a restaurant. Perhaps I should buy food from the sellers who set up shop by the streets. Still living in memory, at night, I'd check out a local nightclub, where the music would be a mixture of western pop and local music, including highlife.

In the mind's mornings, looking at alternatives, depending on where I'd be, the crow of a fowl or the call of Muslims to prayer might wake me up. Nor would I be surprised to hear a Buddhist chanting. On Sundays, in fact most weekdays, I'd find some church service of sorts – from traditional churches, including Catholic and protestant, to more charismatic ones where it is not uncommon to hear local drums and other instruments beating to loud singing and energetic dancing. Even under the siege of things foreign, Ghanaians have a way of domesticating things to make it their own.

These were pleasant recollections, but I also realised that they were dangerous. I would not embrace America properly as I should if I continued to engage in such vivid mental travelling. I decided to try my best to live the present, although I knew this resolve would be tested.

Four

I had my first orientation event the next day, organised by the International Students Association or ISA. Its president, Yannis, welcomed the new group of international students. "This is your mini orientation before The University gets you indoctrinated and disoriented. We figure this way you'd feel first and foremost a part of the ISA. We want you to know we're here for you . . . " With exaggerated gestures, he asked that we remember and never forget who we were. He sounded too clichéd for me. "America will disappoint you at some time," he said, his hand wagging, "but you must know you are stronger than those disappointments." I thought this an odd remark at the time and something close to a dislike for Yannis lodged somewhere in me. As I became more familiar with it, I realised it was a mechanism to deal with an opaque guardedness that Yannis had about him. And perhaps, as later events would validate, he had ample reason to be guarded, especially towards me. He continued, "One thing I ought to let you know is you must always carry cash with you when you go out for a meal, even if someone else has invited you. I remember when I first got here and two American upper classmen invited me to go get some pizza. I was thinking, wow, these guys are so nice. But then when the bill came, they divided it by three and indicated that they were expecting me to pay my share."

"They asked you to pay your share even though they invited you?" a first year student asked.

The lean, shorthaired, intense Yannis smiled. "You can imagine my embarrassment. I had to pretend I'd forgotten my wallet and borrow from one of them, which I repaid later."

After this first lesson in American invitational cultures, we heard from George Mburu, a third year student from Kenya. He said he had every confidence we'd all succeed. He said there were a myriad of resources at our disposal, the ISA being one of them. We shouldn't hesitate to take full advantage. *Okay, Okay, George, but what is it like? How are Americans like?* I was disappointed in what sounded once again like clichéd advice. But much later, I'd understand this sanitised advice, the necessary public façade. Later when we were alone, Mburu said, "Here, you represent all of Africa, all of the black race. They are watching you. Remember that, whatever you do." *Heavy words, George.* As others spoke, my mind wandered. I thought of Mama and Papa, my brothers and sisters. I remembered Marjorie. How I missed her!

After the ISA orientation, we had a general orientation from The University itself at a large gathering dubbed *Know Your University*. It comprised an ocean of people and organizations. From fraternities to social and political clubs, it seemed every voice and organization on campus was represented. On my left was a long array of tables. I saw representatives of the concert band, drama troupes, the student newspaper, the film society, the radio station, several fraternities and sororities and several teams (basketball, ice hockey, lacrosse, sailing, volleyball, swimming, soccer, equestrian, tennis, etc.), among others.

Was this the best way to know The University when each organization seemed in competition with the others and each voice appeared drowned by another? I could barely know The University amid such novelty, human traffic and its attendant cacophony, almost approaching pandemonium in my mind.

I left the event a bit more disoriented (Yannis was right). I had some free time before the next scheduled meeting with the International Students Adviser. I decided to roam the campus a little, move away from the din and explore its silent parts. My pulse must have been pouncing, for there was a lot to take in all at once. I moved away, though temporarily, from the challenge of conversation. Communication, once so easy, continued to be an issue as Americans still spoke too fast for me and overused slang. I had to repeat words and sometimes even spell them to be understood. I especially had a problem with the way *t* almost sounded like *d*, and *a* almost became an *e* – man was almost pronounced as men. Oh my!

I wanted not just to see my surroundings but notice them as well. I started on The University Park, a large spread of immaculately manicured green grass in the middle of campus (crisscrossed by footpaths) that lay like a massive carpet in front of the main campus library. Now in daylight, I noticed its cathedral-like tower that in turn housed a massive hour-chiming clock. I remembered the way it chimed before my first supper on campus the previous evening. In the chill of the early fall, there were a few sunbathers. It had not yet plunged into cold temperatures, but the weather was cooler than I'd ever known. I knew worse was yet to come, as I had been told.

I felt obliged to enjoy what I had before it worsened. I gulped in the smell of the season. I had plenty of time to walk on. I went past the dorm buildings behind the library and came to Fraternity Row, whose buildings boldly displayed their Greek alphabets. Further down the road, I made a turn into woods that suddenly seemed to creep up on me. Past a lonesome stone tower, the pine trees stood tall – here, they owned the land. Inside their enclave was The University Pond. Together, they gave me another smell of the fall: the smell of trees and damp wood, the smell of silence in peace (or peace in silence?) and the naturalness of it – together, an agreeable odour... I was falling in love. I stood there a long while, watching and admiring. The memory of home unfurled again. I could be holding Marjorie's hand, kissing her. I could be speaking with Papa, sharing a meal with Mama, playing soccer with my siblings. Here, time didn't move, it evolved into something that seemed pristine without regard to time, whose passage went almost unnoticed. Here, I was capable of being home, hearing the voices that were familiar, knowing the sounds that were not bound to particular locations, where geographic boundaries were as meaningless as the shape of tears.

I headed back to my room to let simmer and settle the tranquility I'd just experienced. I escaped from it because I feared that if I stayed there too long, I would be spoiled and it would become harder for me to embrace the rest of the campus, which I would have to deal with more regularly. A newspaper lay outside the door to my room. I picked it up and read its title: *The University Review*. I'd read it to relax, I decided. I soon was arrested by one particular caption: Internationalism and Academics.

Hmm...I read on. It surprised me in general, its tone and ideas, but in pertinent part the most stunning was the following paragraph:

> The University celebrates the admission of a Freshman Class of thirty international students from Asia, Africa, Europe and South America. We need not indulge in much imaginative thinking to know that this desire to increase the presence of international students comes, for the most part, at the expense of lowered academic excellence.

Lowered academic excellence? Was that what I was at The University to do? I fell asleep. I was a bit relieved when I discovered later that *The University Review* was neither the official university newspaper nor sanctioned in any way by The University.

That afternoon, I met my faculty adviser, also the International Students' Adviser, in his office. He seemed a timid, cagey man. This wasn't my image of an American man. His body language seemed too laid back, a bit too wimpy for my preconceived expectation. His desk was a clutter of paper and books, like a mirror to the equally booked and papered office. We spoke briefly, how things were unfolding for me generally. He invited me to his home for dinner. "You're the last student I'm seeing today," he explained. We walked there from his office, about five minutes from campus on the outskirts of the town. It was a Victorian mansion reclining behind a creek that rolled leisurely in the front. The pathway towards his home soon became a short bridge overlaying the creek. I crossed the bridge cautiously as what had looked sturdy to me from a distance suddenly seemed shaky once I stepped on it. And every step appeared to make it even more rickety, bringing annoying squeaks. Strange as it seemed, I was grabbed by an awkward fear that the bridge would collapse and plunge me down into the unknown wetness underneath, that I'd never reach his home, that I'd drown trying. I had an uncomfortable urge to turn back. I didn't.

If I could have known his thoughts then (as he would later tell me), I would have learned that he was thinking of the previous evening, when he'd sat outside on his porch, content, except for the one burning ambition to become Dean of Students. Besides that, he couldn't imagine life otherwise, delighted that he so enjoyed the calm around him at that time of day: a faintly glowing sun, the tranquil groan of the creek, the casual movement of birds, leaves occasionally floating fleetingly in the air and even the grass seeming to obey the call of a sudden rush of wind.

At that time, neither of us knew it, but we were connected more than most by the shared tranquility – I by the University Pond and its environs and he by his home and its surroundings. Both of us knew the comfort of home and what either invoked it or found it for us.

If I had shared his thoughts then, I also would've known that as the years grew for him, William Redford's earlier dismissal of such gifts had evolved into an implacable desire to capture the beauty of these things around him, an evolution rooted perhaps in the lessons of age, an ushering of sorts into a yearning to take stock of what he'd missed along the busy years: high school valedictorian achieved through many hours in the library, summa cum laude in college, five years for a PhD and then the years of research to publish and the effort of lecturing and getting tenured. Along the way, he'd gained a wife and two children. Now if only he could be Dean of Students, a position that required political skills rather than hard work... But he was not a man of the world. Where would he summon the political cunning needed to win the position? He could only wait and hope and while he waited, he wasn't to be denied what he could claim. So his evenings were almost invariably preceded by this visit with the outside, sitting on his rocking chair and watching the full emptiness in front of him, his cup of tea carefully balanced in one palm, while he waited for his wife Winnie to return from her downtown job as a legal secretary at Swift and Rich. Her hours there were long. (As I'd learn later, she'd decided to retire in two weeks.)

It was within the context of this near religious serenity that he invited me to visit. Did he have a message there, whether conscious or unconscious? I sat next to him, sharing the cup of tea he'd offered. A tension remained, I could sense. Although one would have thought an International Students Adviser would acquire the skills, he seemed to want to put me at ease without knowing how. He started with what could be the puny transcendent concern of two men: the weather. It was already too cold for me, I said. Wait until the winter comes and you have to deal with the snow and the freezing weather, he said. He asked what I wanted to do. I didn't know yet; no time to hurry, he advised, I had plenty of time. How am I getting along so far? Trying to adjust, I said, but so far so good. I would be fine, he said – in a month, I would be fully settled and behaving as an American. Culture shock? That was a question to be asked at the end of my stay, for the shock, if any, of being exposed to a new culture isn't to be measured in days or weeks or even months, but by the depth of many years accumulated, tasted, tested, weighed, felt, loved, rejected, hated, accepted. (Like getting to know Ed or any person.) But the shorthand for all that, which was an inadequate prologue, was my pleasant response, "I don't think there's been much of a shock yet. I have read so much about America, seen so many American films, I had a sense of what to expect. I'm still finding it difficult to understand the American accent, however, especially American slang."

Very dumb, Jojo. Are you basing your expectations on the distortions of books and movies?

"Give it some time, Jojo."

Winnie Redford emerged on the footpath. Even in the distance, her wrinkled face seemed to belie the strength of inner spirit and the sparkle of voice I would soon hear. When she narrowed the distance, she asked, "What have you boys been up to?"

"Jojo and me were having a bit of a chat."

"Hi Jojo," said Winnie Redford. "Ed told me about you. Welcome to America."

The sky had turned dimmer and sunless, the previously yellow now grey, its illumination quickly burning out. Minutes later, Winnie invited us inside for dinner. As if they knew my preference, the food was spicy. But beyond the physical tastes, theirs was welcome company, especially Winnie's. Still, their warmth was a bit distant, as if guarded – almost like Yannis, although theirs didn't invoke the same negative feelings. Instead, it seemed to suppress spontaneity, request a façade of pleasantry to match theirs, whether or not genuine. Perhaps it was because in some ways I felt like an art piece in a museum: under favourable but curious scrutiny. And so it inhibited spontaneity on both sides, I thought. I learned a bit more about Winnie's work at Swift and Rich, and a little about their boys in college. They conveyed a sense of deep content, as if they'd conquered or accepted all challenges and therefore transcended all that was petty. The grace with which they ate and the calm with which they spoke seemed too casual to be orchestrated solely for my benefit. When I left later that evening, I had made new friends in that, despite my reservations, they made me somewhat comfortable, made me believe in their interest in me, made me believe I could rely on them for help. "Come talk to me if you need anything or if you just want to talk," Winnie Redford had said. I felt I could achieve much at The University (or in America) with such substantive people by my side.

Five

Still, I puffed with emotional exhaustion as I left the Redfords. I had struggled somewhat to maintain decorum at a table foreign and unknown, despite the Redfords' apparent eagerness to put me at ease. Opposites don't always attract, or sometimes not that easily. (Though perhaps it was wrong to think of them as opposites.) I sought silence to recuperate from the emotional exertion, but instead I heard someone call from a moving car: "You want a ride, my brother?" The car moved slowly beside me – at walking pace. A young man looked at me from the driver's seat. "I saw you at Orientation yesterday. I was helping out at the Black Students' desk. You didn't stop by our desk, but that's okay. Too much already to digest in your first week. Get in if you're going up campus. That's where I'm headed."

Once I sat next to him I realised how diminutive his features were (almost like Ed Palmer): a minuscule torso, thin limbs, slender neck peaking into a slightly oversized head. Still, he spoke boomingly and confidently.

"You like it so far?" he asked.

"There's a lot to learn, but so far I'm doing all right."

"Where're you from?"

"Pardon me?"

"Where're you from? You seem to have a funny accent?"

Funny? First strike, my brother.

"I'm from Ghana."

"Ghana. That's Africa, ain't it?"

"Yes."

"I've heard a lot about Africa. Lots of myths and voodoo and crap. Is it true?"

Oh my. Oh my.

"I see."

"What's your name?"

"Jojo Badu."

"Dwayne Dray."

He said he was headed to the Afro-American Society House (or Afro-Am for short), but he needed to stop by a dorm nearby "For a second to see my honey. You don't mind, do you? It'll only take a second."

He returned minutes later arm in arm with a woman. Lean and firm, she approached with dignity, profiled by the moonlight, projecting ease as though sure of everything (although her perfume was heavy and too sharp as would be expected in an overused perfume shop). "Tanya," she said. "Dwayne says you're a freshman?"

"Yes."

"Well, be careful. Don't let them teach you bad habits."

Later, as Dwayne took me to my dorm, he intimated that although he liked Tanya, she didn't like to party. "Always got her head buried in a book." He asked me to join a party at the Afro-Am the next week. But Ed wanted me to go to a frat party with him. "We need to meet some chicks," Ed had said. "I need to get laid." I thought of Marjorie, a strong presence, but was assaulted by a gnawing weakness for female flesh. Any female. I needed some justification. Because I was in a foreign land, betrayal would not have any meaningful impact. I was too far removed from her that whatever I did wasn't consequential, or even important as it would be if it were with a Ghanaian woman. Surely a selfish rationalization without good logic, I realised. But don't they say what we don't know won't hurt us? Marjorie, believing and trusting. How would she know?

And later the following week, two parties with two opportunities . . . I compromised with Ed. I'd go with him to Frat Row but leave early to go to the Afro-Am. We started at the very first fraternity: Kappa Kappa Kappa. It seemed the sole purpose of the large crowd there, mostly in sweatshirts and jeans, was to drink the free beer offered in the basement, which was drunk with abandon and offered in an assortment of drinking games. I found the smell of stale beer unpleasant, compensated only by its abundance. Someone approached me, his appearance so generic that although I knew I'd seen him somewhere, I couldn't be sure. "Hi, I'm John Owens," he said. "You're in my international relations class."

"Jojo," I said.

"Are you thinking of rushing Kappa?"

"What's rushing?"

"Basically trying to join the fraternity."

"Oh . . . I'm not sure. I haven't thought about it."

"I will," he said. "It's a great frat. Anyway, think about it. Talk to you later." John moved away. He seemed to be on a mission, the way he spoke quickly, pronounced his intention and moved on as if to repeat himself to as many would-be Kappa members as he could.

After an hour, composed mostly of Ed trying fruitlessly to seduce a number of women, we left the KKK and went to the next fraternity house. I could tell Ed was getting drunk, as were many others there. After incessant drinking at three fraternities, I had to leave. I was glad. I'd met hardly any women who'd showed even the remotest interest in me. My antennae at that time had not become sharpened enough from the lessons of experience to detect hostility, unless, of course, it was blatantly obvious. But my *otherness* seemed to weigh on me: my manner of speech, the penchant of so many either to ignore me completely or show overt curiosity, the use of slang and phrases I didn't know, the request to repeat my words ... For the first time, I saw myself more sharply in terms of colour as a contrast to others and became self-aware of it in a native way I'd never known before. For the first time I sensed what it must feel like to be one of a kind among others, and not just read about it – the nagging sense of separateness that is not proclaimed but finds its place somewhere in the psyche and somewhere else deeper still: somewhere spiritual, so debilitating, so passively wounding, so dangerous, yet so oddly empowering and even enriching. But now that I was headed for the Afro-Am I would be among my kind. Even if I couldn't claim the American part, I could claim the Afro part.

I therefore went with images of WEB DuBois, Malcolm X, Mohammed Ali and Martin Luther King lingering in my mind, expecting long periods of in-depth, substantive discussion over a glass or two of wine with Louis Armstrong playing in the background (Oh, Satchmo, how Uncle Kusi loved you). I would strip away those inhibiting layers of otherness suffocating me on Frat Row, I would reject the self-awareness and lose myself in the sameness of my colour and by doing so I would be able to reclaim myself.

But when I arrived in the darkened room, a sense of foreboding seemed to spread through me. The music was loud. I believe it was something from The Supremes. The dancing was more frenetic than I could dig. I stood there alone, not knowing what to do or how to engage in the partying. After all, I too wanted to belong, to be hip with the in-crowd. But I was too ill prepared for it, for after propositioning three women to dance and being rejected, I became even more clueless. A shadow among shadows, but a distinct shadow nonetheless. What could I do? Redemption: I saw Dwayne enter the room. "I thought you wouldn't make it," I said.

"No way am I going to miss this. I'm going to make the most of it."

"Where's Tanya?"

"She's in the library. Can you believe it? It's Friday night and she's in the library."

He was gone and in the next instant dancing with a fetching woman, while I kept holding on to walls for long minutes. Here, there was a distance that I couldn't define, and perhaps it was, like air, not definable in its infinite qualities. The distance Frat Row had given me conferred a tangibility I could almost feel and attempt to confront. This, however, had a seamless quality to it, an unforced presence, profiled by the oneness of colour, but each bit, if not more, poignant and the more distressing. I had no idea how this intangible beast became a part of the party. Perhaps I had introduced it and it existed only in my mind. Where was the large black fraternity that might transcend continents, the glue of shared suffering and experiences? How could it be so easily usurped? Or was I being silly by using this party experience as a distorted microcosm of the larger one that was much better than this portrait I was drawing? There was such discomfort I swore I'd never go to an Afro-Am party again, thinking it was better I go where I expected to feel different than where I didn't expect it and felt so anyway.

Ed was already there when I returned to the dorm room, but he wasn't alone. There were five others with him seated in a circle: two women and three men. Bob Dylan's music formed the background to their *meeting*. The smell of marijuana immediately confronted me as they passed the joint among themselves. They were each holding a beer bottle and swinging back and forth. Ed introduced me to his friends. I didn't pay much attention to the men, but the women . . . I tried to stay resolute, but stripped too long of Marjorie's presence, I felt lodging within me a raw attraction to one of them. Phoebe. Phoebe Shaw. Her hair was just as long as Ed's and quite stringy, except she'd tied hers into a ponytail. She moved aside to make room for me to sit. There was something seemingly organic about her, something very natural or rather a forced naturalness, which didn't matter to me at that time. Like Marjorie, but unlike Marjorie. Where was the similarity and where was the difference? Wish it were easy to articulate. It was clear that she wore no bra underneath her tee shirt, which did little to hold her pointed breasts underneath. She had rolled her long dress to her knees, revealing unshaved legs and when she moved her arms up as though to enjoy the music, her unshaved armpits matched the hairy darkness on her legs. Marjorie didn't shave her legs either, but dark hair on dark skin didn't look as awkward as dark hair on light skin. On such full revelation, there was a level of revulsion at Phoebe just as much as there was attraction. She passed the marijuana joint to me. I declined. "Come on," she entreated. Someone said something about not being too square. Phoebe passed her beer bottle to me. I hesitated a moment, undecided. Shall I drink from the same bottle as her? Phoebe almost pushed the bottle into my mouth, leaving me little choice but to accept it. Or rather, my choice seemed constrained by the insistence. As I gulped, they started chanting... Go Go Go... imploring me to finish the half-full bottle in that one gulp. I felt I had to oblige to compensate for declining the joint. I didn't want to be too square, after all. Ed retrieved additional bottles from the fridge and the carouse continued. We chugged down the seemingly endless supply as if we were drinking water. In an hour or so, I was completely inebriated. Through the hazed gaze of alcohol, I saw Phoebe pass me another joint. This time it seemed worth trying. I was too drunk to care. I took some puffs and passed it around. Swimming somewhere higher in my own head, I began to feel sick. I announced that to the group. "You'll be all right. This ain't your first time, is it?" Phoebe asked. "No," I lied. She moved her hand, over my hair, attempting to tousle it – female contact on a vulnerable body. A sensation swelled inside me and I wanted to return the touch, return it to her in an innermost way. And that was the last sensation I remember of that night.

When I woke up the next day I was lying naked in my bed. Ed told me that I'd passed out and they'd carried me into bed. "Who took my clothes off?"

"Phoebe did," he said.

"Are you playing with me?"

"I'm serious. We put you on the bed and came back here. But Phoebe returned to the bedroom. 'To get you more comfortable,' she said."

I wasn't sure whether to thank Ed or slap him. "How could you let her do that?"

"Don't get so worked up," he said. "What do you have to hide? Hey, she was in there a long time. For all I know, she could've been screwing you."

Oh What a Night. My head ached as I went to work in the dish room at the cafeteria. I didn't want to work at that moment, but this work-study was part of my financial aid package and I couldn't afford to jeopardise that.

Six

During class the following Monday, John Owens came late and sat next to me. He fidgeted during the rest of class and invited me to his apartment afterward, saying he had something important to discuss with me. He came from a wealthy background, if his off campus apartment were a testament. When I sat on his couch, I noticed a massive framed painting of a unicorn hanging on the wall facing me. It was an impressive work – a unicorn of unsullied white standing atop a completely blackened mountain. The contrast of colours was striking. John moved over to the painting and adjusted it. "It never seems to hang right," he said. He asked me about doing an interview for *The University Review*. "I want to ask you about how you feel about relationships between Africans and Afro-Americans. I hear you two don't like each other."

"Who told you that? That's just not true. In any case I can't do it, John. For a paper like *The University Review*? That would be a betrayal of my people, wouldn't it?"

"Why? The truth is all I'm asking." He went to readjust the painting. "If you prefer, we can keep it anonymous. No one will have to know that it was you."

"I'm sorry, John. I just can't do it."

And I had reason to reject that request, which if I'd granted would be nothing more than racial apostasy, if you ask me. Yet his assertion seemed germane. I felt naked; it seemed my innermost thoughts exposed when I didn't so wish. Not that he was right. He'd said we didn't *like* each other. Speaking for myself, that wasn't true, but had he not come too close to the truth? It wasn't *dislike*, but what was it? I was ashamed of the beast that had gnawed at me at the Afro-Am party. I was so ashamed that John knew (or suspected it) that I wanted to eliminate all remnants of it. Yet this was a beast I couldn't kill by myself. It was as if it had multiple lives and would require many slayers.

But it so happened that, even without my input, the article would be published the next week. In pertinent part, it read:

> Have you ever paused a minute to ponder the phenomenon of intra-racial prejudice? The whole world proselytises against racial prejudice, the *cause celebre* of the so-called black consciousness movement. But how about black on black prejudice? Let us set aside the varying degrees of prejudice by Negroes against each other based on shades of skin colour. There exists another mutation of black against black discrimination that remains ignored.
>
> Have you ever stopped a minute to ask an African student on campus how he feels about Afro-American students and *vice versa*? Last month, I was tipped off by an African student – who asks for anonymity in fear of the ostracism that will otherwise follow – of the frustration of Africans on campus. Africans are frustrated because they do not quite fit in with white students. At the same time, they can find no sanctuary among American

> Negroes because the latter, for one reason or the other, tend to deprecate their African counterparts.
>
> A number of Africans feel that black Americans relegate them to second-class status. Says one African student, "American blacks don't like us because we represent everything that they don't want to be, everything the society has taught them they have to run away from. They blame us for befriending white students, but they don't accept us as we are. In fact, I find more white than black American students interested in my background in Africa. Some of them even continue to blame us for selling their ancestors into slavery. Perhaps I simplify. It is a complex relationship, but one thing is for sure: it is not an easy relationship." As it stands, it seems a lot of enmity has been generated on campus among black students, at least among the Africans towards black Americans.

Dwayne called me. "Brother, what's going on?" He was enraged.

"What do you mean?"

"*You* tell me! What's this I just read in *The University Review*? What have you been telling them?"

"Me? Telling them? What makes you think I've been telling them anything?"

"You're saying you haven't spoken with them?"

"That's exactly what I'm saying."

"Well, one of you Africans have."

"What makes you say that? Don't you think it could all have been made up?"

"No way some of this could've been just made up. Someone told. If you feel that way, why can't you talk to me? Did you have to go talk to them? Come on, Jojo. Talk to me. Brother to brother. I don't care if it's the way *you* feel. If even one African on campus feels that way, I want to know. Do you...I mean do some Africans on campus really feel that way?"

"There's some truth in it, you know. How come more white students seem interested in me, my background? Why do I have more white than Afro-American friends?"

"Are you fooled by these white boys and their girls? You think it's because they love you or because they see you as an exotic object of interest? Like a mascot, a curiosity..."

"I don't know, Dwayne. I can't assign motive, ill or not. I can't read minds. I can only react to what I know, what I see, what I hear."

"Well, perhaps you should give it a bit more thought, assign motives. Think history, your history, my history, our history and experience with white folks. Put it in that context."

"Our history? Dwayne, yours and mine are very different."

"What are you talking about? Black history is what it is."

"Yes, but where does it converge and where does it diverge? We have to admit that at least...we have to recognise the differences between us...the Diaspora and the mother continent. I didn't before, not when I first arrived in this country, but I think I'm learning. I am learning to accept that I am African and you are American and that we will be connected by ancestry, colour, but that we are also different. You were born here, raised here. There is an American prism that affects your view of things, no matter how it may be affected by your qualified status as an Afro-American. Your Afroness is qualified and influenced by your American-ness. For me, the prism is African, Ghanaian. If we expect sameness from each other, we will forever be in friction."

Dwayne didn't reply for seconds. "Well, then," he said after a while, "can you try and see where I'm coming from and perhaps I too try and understand you?"

"Sure, Dwayne."

"But you know what's really sad?" he asked. "A white boy's article got us into this conversation."

Dwayne invited me to listen to Martin Luther King's *I Have a Dream* speech in his dorm. I was obliged to accept the invitation and I was glad I did. Hardly had I seen a public figure display such eloquence, grace, charisma and sheer conviction. I was moved. "I too have a dream," Dwayne said after the speech. "It is a dream rooted in a World Dream. I have a dream that someday the children of Afro-American blacks will hold hands with the children of Africans and proclaim *free at last, thank God almighty, we are free at last.*"

Next time we met he'd invited me to a football game with his girlfriend Tanya. "Don't you want privacy?"

"You're crazy? Privacy at a football game?"

"I don't understand the game."

"I'll show you what it's all about."

I was bored in the beginning, as watching oversized men crowd around, make noises, line up, throw balls, catch balls, get hit and fall mightily didn't appeal to me. Where was the grace and skill of real football, which Dwayne insisted wasn't football at all but soccer? "American football is the real thing, brother," he said. Dwayne was too involved in the game to explain it to me, happy to relinquish that task to Tanya. It was libidinal, not spiritual, my interest in Tanya – not the way I felt with Marjorie. I needed some release. I was finding attractive just about any woman who paid me the slightest attention. Between Dwayne and Tanya, she was, in my reasoning, the calmer of the two, and the more patient. She explained every move, every call, every stop and start. I was continuing to fall in lust with Tanya. She seemed without pretense, so genuine and loving and lovable. I wanted to return that love, even though I knew hers was not lustful. What unknown territories lay behind that sweetness? What pleasures underneath that charm? An unknown sense told me she knew my interest – and enjoyed it. Temptation! But two things forestalled me: my conscience (because she was Dwayne's girlfriend) and my lack of guts (because she overwhelmed me).

By the second half, I was following the action and a bit more interested in the game. After it was over, they invited me to Tanya's room. There, Dwayne insisted I had to find an American woman. "I have a girlfriend at home."

"Come on, you think she's just waiting for you?"

"Sure, she is."

He asked Tanya to set me up with one of her friends.

"Do you want me to, Jojo?" she asked.

"Sure he wants you to," Dwayne said.

"Won't you let the man speak for himself?"

"He's going to act all shy and shifty. Just do it."

"All right, all right . . . I'll introduce him to Deirdre."

"Hell, no! Not her."

"What's wrong with Deirdre?"

"She's butt ugly. I'm gonna have to set him up myself."

I didn't want to overstay my welcome. I left them without thinking much about Dwayne's promise. But a week later he came knocking. "Hey, Jojo," he said, "I've got something for you to do." He wouldn't tell me what. He walked outside, I followed. Dwayne eyed me mischievously, maintaining a disquieting silence. We emerged on The University Park. For a while we stood motionless, simply squinting into the open air. The park was unusually busy at that time, as students roamed it, mostly drenched in sweat from the non-seasonal heat. Here, boys displayed upper naked torsos and the fat and muscles that embroidered them and girls showed as much of their legs and chests as seemed allowable. A lady approached us, rising from a bench nearby. A sudden gush of wind ventured into her skirt and lifted it slightly, briefly exposing her thin thighs. "What do you think?" Dwayne asked me.

"She's not bad," I said.

He snapped, "What're you talking about? This sister is *fine*."

Dwayne walked towards her and whispered in her ear. Soon, they were talking like old acquaintances, but outside my earshot. Dwayne threw his arms around, shifted his body in different poses, rapidly wore and discarded varying facial expressions as if he was trying to impress an important point. They both looked in my direction, slightly embarrassing me. They started walking towards me. I studied her. Her hair was so closely cropped that I could almost see her scalp. Like Marjorie, the little she had glistened under the sun's brightness. Her forehead was broad and her eyebrows appeared to have been brushed over a long time into perfect place. She was lithe by my measure, but projected strength and pulchritude.

She came closer and smiled. I did too. Simultaneously we clasped hands. "Joan," she said. "And you call yourself?"

"Actually, I don't call myself."

She laughed at my caricature of a clichéd joke. "I love your voice. It's so . . . so strong."

Dwayne insisted that we sit for a while. I didn't want to seem interested, mindful of the need to show loyalty to Marjorie. *Darling, they are putting too much pressure on me.* We sat, the three of us and spoke for at least an hour. As we were parting, Joan said, "There's a party at the University Commons on Saturday. Want to come with me?"

"Yes." *Forgive me.*

I could hardly void my mind of Joan the next few days, which reduced me to a sweet-misery, a mysterious excitement. An American woman for me! How could I not embrace the excitement? *Sorry, Marjorie, the invitation is too enticing.* I tried to plan every move of the coming seduction, yet I hadn't a clue. I was on *terra nova* but refused to compromise my pride by asking Dwayne or Ed for help.

I went to fetch Joan at her dorm room and we walked together to the University Commons. I had the first dance with her and then she got too busy: one man after another asked to dance with her and she obliged them. She would come to me between dances, puffing and sweating and asking, "Are you having fun?" Obliging the polite voice in me, I said the expected "Yes," my impression being that she didn't realise what she was doing. I suspected that Joan was in a constant state of fantasy, which she assumed everyone shared with her, for how could she not discern my misery in seeing her yield one after the other to every male's request to dance? Their language, again, being too glib for me to imitate, I felt the outsider looking in, helpless to arrest the tide. My imagined seduction stayed imaginary – mind proposes, reality disposes. But shouldn't I have blamed myself? What was I doing here when

Marjorie held my bond, my covenant to remain faithful, sealed by blood?

Joan asked that I walk her home when the party ended. I felt incapable, dwindled out of her league. I had not a chance. But I played the gentleman, walking her to her door and bidding her goodbye. "Not even a kiss?" she asked. "Oh, you Africans."

How could she expect a kiss when she'd hardly paid any attention to me all night? I obliged her with a kiss, a long tongue ballet. Now she had me aroused, ready to consummate what she had so strongly awoken. I reached for the straps of her dress, my conscience (in light of Marjorie) killed by this lustful drive. But she stopped me. "No, I have to wake up early tomorrow. Goodnight." What kind of teasing was that? Is this how American women are? I wondered. To lead you to the brink and not let you fall in, seeing the mighty rivers and not swimming? I left with a swollen penis. Given that she seemed so friendly with other men, given the alienation she made me feel when with her in the company of others, I decided I better not expect anything from her. I made no attempt to pursue her. Perhaps it was fear, perhaps it was my conscience reawakened. I tried to avoid her, as she always reminded me of failure. Exactly what the failure was, I couldn't grasp. It wasn't the failure to bed her, for that feeling dissipated with the night. Might it have been all those men I saw her with, who seemed to be so easeful in her company and she with them? Was it that her attraction continued to nag me even as I tried to ignore her? Attraction, that beguiling phantom that is now here, now gone, now strong, now weak. Was it deceiving me into thoughts of failure because I couldn't or wouldn't pursue her as I was expected to? Was I just too weak for not trying (whatever the legitimacy of the reason)? Joan left me exhausted with thought. Unable to resolve Joan, I imagined Phoebe instead. What had happened the night she undressed me? Had she, as Ed half-jestingly suggested, taken my manhood into her while I lay unconscious? The image was pregnant enough to birth further images of her, a fully clothed, hairy woman, white as air, bent over my prostrate body, her body drinking from its dark spouts as I still lay drugged unconscious but alive. If it was a mere imagination or a reality reconstructed, I didn't know. But I journeyed joyously in the thought that it could have happened, making me wonder what it would be like to bed Phoebe or one like her.

When I next saw Joan she was eating solo in the dining room. I was with a couple of my friends. She eyed me without acknowledging my greeting, as if I'd done something awful that required recrimination. That was sufficient thought to keep me thinking all through lunch. From time to time, I tried furtively to observe her. I knew she knew I was pilfering occasional glimpses, but she did not look in my direction once. I was intrigued by her behaviour. I wanted to ask her why. I waited until lunch was over. "Hello," I said.

She looked up at me. "Yes?"

I was even more puzzled. "Is something wrong?"

"Huh?"

"You ignore me."

She shrugged. This was cruel. Indifference gestured, not even spoken; at best, ambiguity well controlled.

I went on, "Why?"

"What do you want from me?" Words at last.

I couldn't believe the pretense – as if nothing had happened before. What of the mighty kiss? "Joan . . . I thought . . . "

"You thought what?"

My pride had suffered enough. "I'll see you later." She said nothing.

I left her, even though thoughts of her remained. At work that evening in the kitchen, the heat of the dishwashing machine unfavorably encircling me, dishes coming at speed over the conveyor belt as I tried to toss wasted food off the plates, the stereo in the room blasting at full volume, I thought of Joan. As I fed the machine, unloaded and cleaned the tops of plates and wiped them, as well as the sweat on my face, I thought of Joan. Later, as I studied for my class quizzes, I thought of Joan. Could I ever have her? Occasionally I managed to replace the recurring image of Joan with Phoebe's. I wrote a series of letters to Marjorie in a mighty outburst of emotionally charged literary energy.

When I next saw Joan, she was walking to class as I was, only in the opposite direction. After her last rejection, I was disinclined even to acknowledge her. "Jojo!" she yelled, and then with a softened voice added, "How are you?" She was smiling at me: a large, seemingly genuine smile; a bright infectious smile that gladdened my heart. I would have liked to mimic her treatment of me, but I couldn't because of the way she projected her warmth to me, hugging me even. "How've you been?" she restated her question.

"I'm doing well," I said with a slight hint of restored pride.

"Haven't seen you in a long time. We should do something one of these days, you know. Like go see a movie or go out to dinner or something."

"Sure," I said, though afraid to turn the suggestion into an invitation. She didn't either.

"I'll call you or something," she said. Or something: a negation expressed as a positive and the more deceitful because of its ambiguity.

"Okay."

She rubbed my cheeks. "You take care." Hope rekindled.

"I'm falling in love," I told Ed, but was I?

"Go for it."

When I told Dwayne in Tanya's presence, he encouraged me, but she suggested I forget Joan. Her friend Deirdre would be a better match. Against Dwayne's protestations she invited Deirdre to have lunch with us. Now, trying to be polite, I have searched the dictionary for an alternative word to best describe Deirdre without sounding cruel. Alas, I must say, there's only one word that best describes her: ugly. (Notice that I have generously withheld the word hideous, though it could be applied.) Capitalise and underscore ugly and put it in bold and hang it out. That was Deirdre. But she was one of the nicest persons I'd ever met. It wasn't forced, either. There was a natural ease and pleasantness about her that ought to have overshadowed the ugliness and in a small measure, it did. But how does one really fail to react to that ugly face, atop an ugly neck sitting over a completely misshapen body?

"What do you think?" Tanya asked me later on.

"She's nice."

"I told you she's nice. She likes you. You think you'd like to go out with her?"

"I'm not sure."

"Why not?"

"Because she's ugly, that's why," Dwayne rescued me.

"Come on, guys, she's a great girl..." None of us responded. "Oh well, I tried."

But my hope in Joan was misplaced. She was like sun and moon. Sometimes she shunned me completely; sometimes she embraced me with niceties. I couldn't tell which version of her I'd encounter or when. Because of that uncertainty, I had something akin to fear of her, found her more and more attractive and pined to be with her, but detested her because of her double-edged treatment. She was an enigma beyond my understanding.

I sought Mburu's advice at the next International Students Association party. "She's bad news. Leave her alone."

"But she's so pretty."

"Don't let that fool you. She's got a reputation for being bitchy."

Was that all the fault he could find? I was willing to live with *bitchy* if Joan would just let me into her realm, even if to its fringes. I craved her. I wasn't sure if this was love or a desire to solve a riddle that seemed unsolvable.

Yannis came around asking if we were enjoying the party. I answered politely, fighting hard to shed my dislike of him. The main event comprised a poetry reading by an ISA member from Bangladesh and sitar playing by an Indian followed by an Indian dance they called *kuchipudi*. Before the night closed, Yannis invited me to the next ISA meeting. "You don't want to miss this one," he said. "If you can only come to one ISA meeting, this should be it." The way he said it, I knew he was planning something important. I asked him, but he wouldn't say. It was a month away and he already had me eager and impatient. I hated the bastard for it.

I struggled to stay faithful to Mburu's advice. As it was, my days got even busier as classes became more intense, midterm exams approached and I juggled this with work in the dish room. Not that I worked long hours, but they were physically exhausting. The first midterms were intense. "Don't take them for granted," Mburu advised. "You've got to study hard. Show them what we Africans are made of." I studied hard, perhaps harder than needed and was exhausted. It was after that that my dorm organised its post-midterm party. It was opened to all. Beers and mixed, often vile, liquors were abundant. Ed was drunk within minutes and puking within an hour. I drank a little more slowly, but under the encouragement of my dorm mates, I too was gone soon enough and puking as well. I didn't remember much of it after the first regurgitation. I only remember liquor and vomit and vague matters, like Ed telling me, "I'm going to get laid tonight." I'd heard that before and didn't believe it, based on his track record. I attempted conversation with some of the women. I knew I was incomprehensible. I would later remember a kiss on the cheek, more like a kiss of sympathy rather than desire and then everything was a blur, except the reborn image of Phoebe and me. Where was she, anyway? I must have made it to my bed and passed out as that's where I woke up, fully clothed. The next morning, the bathroom was full of vomit and half empty glasses of beer, some spilled on the floor. The intolerable smell of stale vomit, spit and beer was nauseating. I could barely stand it enough to brush my teeth and rush out, my head aching, hoping that the janitor would clean the mess sooner than later. I pitied her. I noticed Ed sprawled on the couch in the living room. "So did you get laid?"

"This place is insane. I don't know what a guy has to do to get some."

And this was supposed to be the era of free sex. Some kind of sexual revolution for me...

I went to William Redford's, having earlier accepted an invitation from Winnie. The bridge to his home still seemed infirm. Why couldn't he just fix the damn thing? Or was it not so easily done? It was a short lunch and the Redfords seemed more relaxed than before. I met Phoebe on my way back. "I'm going to a rally downtown," she said. "You wanna come?"

"No."

"Come on, Jojo."

"I'm exhausted, Phoebe."

"It won't take long. Come on."

I saw little way to wiggle out. She slid her fingers into mine as we walked to the rally. (Why was she holding my hand? Was she verifying Ed's account of the night I first met her?) I didn't even know what the rally was about, but it wouldn't matter. The closeness to Phoebe seemed ample reason. She was too casual about it though, the way she might hold a brother.

Jim Swift, the rally's organiser, a giant of a man, walked confidently towards the podium as the sun beat on his neck and glistened on his face. He adjusted his tie and smiled as the applause rose from the crowd. His smile seemed to blossom into a grin as though he was the true embodiment of the introductory remarks lauding his achievement as outstanding citizen, accomplished lawyer and philanthropist. I saw Winnie Redford in the crowd. She walked over. "I worked for Mr Swift before I retired," she said. Why hadn't she invited me to the rally?

Or did she think it inappropriate? I introduced her to Phoebe, as Jim Swift began to speak.

"Ladies and gentlemen," he said, "as president of the Association for the Underprivileged, I am very pleased to be here with you today." A ripple of applause rose and intensified. Jim Swift held out his hand to indicate that he wanted quiet, but the crowd ignored him for a full minute. "I am particularly pleased because we are here in honour of a great cause. Let me begin first by thanking you all for coming to help raise funds for the underprivileged, those who cannot afford the basic necessities of life. In a small town like ours, it is difficult to appreciate the problem. We tend to be a very blessed community. But you don't have to travel far from here to some of our bigger cities to see the afflictions some of our fellow citizens face – homelessness, say. Let's not be tempted by our own luxury to ignore these less fortunate people. I say it's not right for us to live large while others live so small. Let's give and give generously."

Jim Swift went on for a while, touching, incongruously it seemed, on the need to protest unjust wars like the Vietnam War, before concluding, "So I say as human beings it is our moral responsibility to help our less privileged friends. As president of the Association for the Underprivileged, I call on you now to do this three mile walk with me, a walk to show our dedication to the cause and draw attention to the plight of those we want to help so that others might get involved. As you all can judge from my frame, this walk is not an easy undertaking for me." Invoking laughter from the crowd, Jim Swift descended from the podium. I thought well of him for his compassion. Phoebe held my hand as we walked on and Winnie winked at me as if to say, *What are you up to*?

Seven

At the next ISA meeting, which he'd made me anticipate so much, Yannis called matters to order to determine what new name would be assigned the Brewer House for International Students. I was relaxed amid familiar people, voices and accents. After all, here's where I felt most comfortable, not due to the politics, which never really appealed to me, but the people I'd met. They were so diverse, so interesting, so boring, so exciting, so smart, so stupid, so cosmopolitan, so bucolic, so sophisticated – a group as united in its *alien* solidarity as much as it was divided by its cultural differences. Here, the world was a microcosm relived in the portion of the student body designated by its hosts as *alien*. Here, aliens met and spoke to each other, but even here, there was alienation within. Aliens among aliens. The Indians kept together more than they interacted with the Pakistanis and vice versa; the Africans were more comfortable with one another than with the Mexicans and vice versa; the bulk of the Europeans hardly mixed with the rest of the group. This was, it appeared, a preferred sub-alienation. Although social interaction was commonplace, certain other things seemed taboo. For example, inter-group dating was rare. And yet within this intricate makeup of unspoken dos and don'ts were occasional exceptions. It would be difficult to draw a straight line through this matrix – the zigzagging was undeniable. But the common glue was the alienation imposed on us all, which therefore guaranteed a sort of charming solidarity within the international students, so that one could relax on the sofa and watch television with students from Malaysia after a meal of *nasi dagang* and curry tuna fish; or spiced *ceviche* with its onions, garlic and red peppers; or share in Mburu's favourite of *ugali* or *chapati* that he liked to serve with hot stew. Within this group, I too found some kind of refuge. On many occasions, I would saunter to the Brewer House for International Students and hold long conversations. There was always someone there, no matter the time as it also doubled as a residential house for some of the students. How could I not be drawn to this place where I could kick off my shoes and lie on the sofa, where I wasn't too concerned who might catch me picking my nose or when a careless fart might escape me?

I had been invited several times to the ISA meetings where they discussed the state of international students on campus and devoted some time as well to political matters. I had never gone, more concerned with my quest to become familiar with Americans and things American. But after Yannis's impassioned request, I felt obliged to attend. I was intrigued as I was hoping to get to like Yannis. What a day I'd chosen.

Unknown to me, a clamour for change had gathered speed and caught up with unfolding events. Brewer House, which we'd all enjoyed, now stood on the precipice of infamy. ISA history was about to be buried (or perhaps reborn after a dormant period). Brewer House, where we'd gathered in our foreign-ness to commiserate, share meals and find routes to connect to one another; where romances were made and split, friendships nurtured and deserted, debates made and aspirations shared, hoarded a secret that was about to erupt like lava. It had a name and like all things with a past, a history that shadowed the present. And now had come the day to wrestle from the building the name, revealed like a sordid detail from the past: Charles Brewer was a slave owner who'd made a large donation to The University. That was the extent of the detail. Someone had actually taken the time to research the name. This, after all, was a time of agitation and unrest, when all things were open to scrutiny. Yannis called a group together and promulgated his findings. "When we found out, it was as though The University was holding us in contempt by granting as the gathering home of its international students a building named after a man who had owned slaves." (Although this fact seemed the prevailing point, what would we have done if it were named Thomas Jefferson or even George Washington, say? Brewer seemed unsung and therefore, an easy target.)

Yannis was gesturing, yelling almost: "We can't allow ourselves to be insulted by such viciousness. Can you believe it? That these urchins will ask us to live in a building named after a slave owner?" The ISA erupted with moans of disgust.

One student, bespectacled and soft spoken, stood up amid the formless clamour, her voice shaking with nerves and attempted a defense. "Should it really matter to us? As we are just guests in this country, should we worry what buildings are named after whom?"

"Nonsense!" Yannis exploded. "What utter nonsense is that?" I hated Yannis for this outburst. Was this really necessary? Ought we not to engage in more civil discourse?

She tried to counter, but the vocal rejection of her only mounted in the room. "Sit down!" someone even yelled from among the group without showing his face. There appeared to be genuine anger, unleashed and worsened now by what seemed an unsustainable apology. Her voice certainly couldn't match the surrounding vehemence. The mounting tension couldn't be stopped, just channelled into a different energy. Yannis did that by asking for a vote on the name. "I propose we vote to change the name to the Fidel Castro House." He truly was taking his current while it served.

And the chorus that followed was booming. "Let's take the vote! Let's take the vote!" The force of the mob, whether reasonable or not, was unleashed and mischief would have to take what course it willed. I knew even then that this was the brewing pot of controversy. At that time, to name a building in a prestigious American university after Fidel Castro, was as daring as it was defiant. It wouldn't matter what the name was being changed from if Castro was what it would become. Another student stood, his voice visibly shaking from the isolation of his position within the crowd, (to me, he seemed bold after what had happened to the earlier voice of dissent). "How can we even think it? How can we name this house after Fidel Castro? Don't..."

"Sit down, motherfucker!" A voice that might have been Yannis's yelled – for he had set the tone and others followed. At first, this was a solo voice, perhaps because it stunned the group with its boldness, but then it was joined by a large number of students shouting "Sit down! Sit down!"

The dissenter did, seeming bewildered by the angry chant. And then when the expurgation ended, someone seconded Yannis's move to take the vote. I didn't know how to vote. I was caught in that tide of revolutionary fervour, in rebellion and resistance, in the passion and energy of the moment, but I was restrained somewhat by the inevitable anger I knew it would create. I tried to rely on my conscience, but it too was as jumbled as my fears. The others must have known it too, but some of them would relish the confrontation. When I put paper to pen, I drew a zero, a neutrality that was in fact a nothingness, like Joan's "something," a betrayal of emptiness (or rather a tribute to it), for I had nothing to offer. No *Yes* or *No* for me. Minutes later, the votes were counted. The International Students Association had just voted by a ninety-five per cent margin to rename its meeting place the Fidel Castro House. The first salvo had just been fired. How far would it resound? Troubled, I left and went to troubled sleep.

That night, as I later learned, a group of international students stripped the shingle hanging from the front of the International Students House and marched to The University president's residence. They held the inanimate object as if it were a sacrificial animal, pulling on it, from time to time stepping and spitting on it. Brewer was theirs to destroy. And they also carried a black cross. It seemed this was not a spontaneous outburst from the energies of the moment, but a preplanned action. "We shall overcome!" they sang underneath black hoods donned over their heads, possessed by the indomitable spirit of protest. From his front yard, they demanded to see the president with loud yells hurled at his residence. It was almost midnight. Either as an act of foolish bravery or misguided trust in his students, the president stepped out to confront them. At first, he showed just concern as a father would over an unknown tremour suddenly seizing his children. But because he didn't know the force of the tremour, he was unprepared to deal with it. He might as well have bared his naked vulnerability to them. Underneath the calmness was the casual roots of authority that hinge on arrogance, a familiarity with subservience that assumes too much; but boldness that dissolves outside its tight familiar funnel. There, under the moon glow, they presented him with the shingle bearing the name of Charles Brewer and told him he could hang it on his residence if he so chose, but no way was it going to continue to foul the International Students House. He might as well have *been* Charles Brewer, for in their vision at that moment, he was no different, be it kinship acquired through colour, silence or indifference. If he presided over such an atrocity, he was the atrocity. They continued to yell at him when he expected a calm conversation, even debate. The president, apparently shaken, asked for names. He got none as by then his authority had shrunk before the students, even if for that moment only. He asked for calm, he got none either as students hollered about The University's retention of such racist legacies. And then the revelation was made to him: "We have renamed the International Students House the Fidel Castro House."

"What?" A '*What?*' restrained by dawning fear. The president was diminished (in his own mind, at least) and appeared wounded, helpless and susceptible – a bleeding worm amid hungry sharks. The momentary loss of power perplexed him and the situation escaped his control. His vulnerability became even more pronounced. This was serious stuff. Fidel Castro? But perhaps more seriously, the students planted the black cross in his yard, despite the president's feeble protests, doused it with gasoline and set it on fire. The president recoiled, holding the shingle as though it were a delicate child. He was completely without ammunition as he headed back to his residence, pale as the moon that lay lonely in the dark night. By the time the campus police arrived, not a single student stood in the yard. The police gazed at a lone black cross burning blacker still. They too seemed wounded, helpless and susceptible.

Much later after subsequent events happened, Professor Redford told me about them as he had either heard or witnessed them unfold. The president of The University summoned the president of the International Students Association to find the details. The two presidents were firm but honest with each other; yet at that moment, neither knew which of them was the more powerful. Was it the one who led the entire university or the one who led a faction that had in the eyes of the other become wayward, loose, untamed and dangerous, a poison that could ooze outward? Poison, after all, didn't need to acquire the size of its victim as a tiny drop could cause such rippling damage. The student president told what had happened. The International Students House no longer answered to a slave owner, but a liberator. The other president was infuriated and needed action. For the moment, though, he was stalled, unsure. The next person he summoned was International Students Adviser William Redford.

"Did you know anything about this outrage, William?"

"No," said a shaken William Redford. "I'm just finding out myself."

"And what do you propose we do about it?"

"We just ignore it. It will pass like anything else so foolish."

"What, William? We can't take this sitting down. I want the vote withdrawn and I want it done immediately. Do you know how outrageous this is? Do you realise how it will look to the outside world? I will have no choice but to take very serious disciplinary action unless something happens, something dramatic. I want a recantation and an apology from the International Students Association! I want the cross burners dismissed!"

"But how do you propose we do that? As I understand it the vote was almost unanimous."

"Find a way, William! Find a way! I want this thing dealt with before the week is over."

William, charged to find a way; William, eyeing the soon-to-open position of Dean of Students and not wanting to rile the man he believed could grant him that job; William, perplexed by the audacity of the act, concerned that the organization he advised could prove his undoing. William was thinking. How was he to deliver this miracle in a climate charged so heavily with rebellion and with history made to stand on its head? It was a challenge that in his mind could do or undo his march to become Dean. Thus charged, he had to excel at the task. He had no choice. He was obsessed with the challenge but he couldn't mould the solution in his mind. This endeavour, like a minefield, seemed so fraught with unseen dangers. The first day came and went and he still hadn't found a solution, though he craved one, not until he passed me by in the library, his head bent low, forehead furrowed with concern, shoulders bowed with what I considered defeat: clearly a body and mind weighed down by absorbing thought. And in my polite way I said hello to him. I said it twice before he could snap from his tunnelled concern and that was when it occurred to him that there was a way out.

His mind worked quickly once the idea came to him: I would lead that egress from the tunnel, he decided. He greeted me in return and said nothing more at the time. But that afternoon, I got the summons to his office. He made no attempt, despite his penchant for diplomacy and ambiguity, to disguise his purpose.

"Jojo," he welcomed me with the legendary firm American handshake that left my hand smarting a little. "I need your help with this imbroglio that the international students have stirred."

"Imbroglio, professor?"

"Yes... Yes... You can understand that The University can't allow this to stand. I just read the story in the *New York Times*. Can you believe that it's already made it to the *New York Times*? How they got wind of it, I don't know. The school is getting some very bad publicity for this mess the ISA has created." I noticed he didn't mention the cross burning. Deliberate error? Omission or commission? "Castro? Here's a man who stands for everything anti-American. I need not repeat what he's done, seizing American property... and don't forget the ignominy of the Bay of Pigs fiasco. Jojo, even the US government will be furious with us if we let this stand. Now, we all have our interests here. As adviser to the ISA, I have my responsibility. I must preserve the name and face of The University. You must help your friends at the International Students Association before this thing goes too far. Who knows what kind of anti-American charges may be leveled against the international students involved in this? Who knows what claims of conspiracy may be leveled against the ISA? And who knows at what level that might happen? You, I know, are the voice of reason. I know you're tactful and sharp. I need you to prevail on the international students to do two things."

"Me?"

"You must renounce this name change, reverse the decision and render an apology to The University."

"Me?"

"I don't mean you personally. I'm talking about the International Students Association."

"But I'm not the one to make that decision."

"I understand that, but you are part of the ISA. You have friends in the ISA. You can talk to those spear-heading this thing. Apply your diplomacy, Jojo. You've got what it takes. I mean, who could tell whether this mess could be deemed seditious... or I mean whatever. You know, I can't guarantee anything. And you know how The University has been generous with its financial aid package. Can The University continue to maintain such aid if the screws begin to tighten from Washington? And believe me, it will if nothing happens and this thing stands."

Three words hammered at me: group, conspiracy and sedition. And looming behind it was financial aid. I was at The University on financial aid (loans, grants and work-study). I couldn't believe those words had been used so carelessly, interspersed though they were throughout the short speech. And come to consider it, I was a member of the International Students Association. Group – guilty as charged. I was there when the vote was taken, even though I'd not voted for it. But how could I prove that in a secret ballot? Maybe, guilty as charged. Conspiracy – could be guilty, depending on who interpreted the facts. And could it not be argued that given the recent historic tension and attempted ostracism of Cuba such an open endorsement of its leader was directly counter to the stated interests of the United States and therefore even against its stability? Sedition – perhaps a stretch, but in a time of nervous nationalism, could be guilty as charged. Financial aid – without it, I couldn't afford to continue at The University. Maybe it was fear or even something more – plain paranoia – but he had my attention.

"What are you proposing, sir?"

"I want your leadership. I will do what I can to get you the support of the other ISA members. I want you to lead the ISA to a vote that reverses its decision. Now, I'm a reasonable person. I know the name Brewer offends most people, so I'm not asking you to go back to that name. The vote will simply revoke the Fidel Castro name and rename the building the International Students House until such time as The University renames it. And finally, I want you to seek a vote calling for an apology to The University. Now, I'm not seeking humiliation here. All I want is for you to state that the ISA apologises for having attempted to change the name if its house without going through the proper channels. I also want the ISA to apologise for other acts on the night of the vote inconsistent with civility." So that's what he preferred to call it: acts inconsistent with civility.

"This is a difficult task, sir. The vote was..."

He smiled. "I won't throw you to the wolves without help. You will have enough votes to prevail. Trust me. I guarantee you that."

And he did, but not without leaving me to sweat under the spectre of ostracism. How could I defy the International Students Association with the call he demanded? And if I did, how would I ever be able to reenter the building, or commingle with the people there? Much as I disliked Yannis and would have liked an opportunity to oppose him, this was not the fight I wanted. It was a very heavy burden, but it was countervailed by the threat William Redford had so deftly and implicitly shot at me. Whether from weakness or self-preservation, I had to find a way. My strategy was simple and probably flawed, yet it was that simplicity that would rescue it (in addition, of course, to the help from William). In the same way William had targeted me, I would reach out to the more moderate members of the ISA. A gamble, a risk, but what choice did I have? The first person I called was Jose, a quiet and retiring Peruvian student. Plus, he was active in the Latin American Students Association as its vice president. He rejected my suggestion. I called ten others, only one agreed with me.

I was defeated. I called William Redford. "I'm getting nowhere," I told him.

"With whom have you spoken?"

Guilty as I felt, I divulged the names. And within a day, I was deluged with phone calls. No less than thirty (out of an ISA population of about seventy). We were getting close. Jose, obviously having changed his mind, suggested we call an emergency meeting of the ISA. He would guarantee the full attendance of members of his association. The meeting would be fully attended. It was scheduled to be held in two days.

Yannis was furious, looking as though he could do murder, sternly eyeballing us one after the other. How dare we do this? Despite my dislike for him, I could empathise with his fury and if circumstances were otherwise I'd wish for his success. But circumstances not being otherwise, I had to hold firm when he confronted me. "We need to reconsider this decision," I said. "It was too rash." But my reasoning would not quench an anger stemming from what he perceived as a direct threat to his authority, a betrayal rooted in his belief that a united front in favour of a morally superior cause was being perverted by pressure from outside the ISA. But whether he liked it or not, there was a movement underway he couldn't control. The president of the university held more strings than the president of the ISA. There was no room for manoeuvre when the strings were so securely controlled. The greater puppeteer was at work. Despite Yannis's frantic appeals and protests, the meeting ensued as scheduled. He held in his anger, but it was clear that it was only a matter of time before it spilled over.

The meeting was tense. Uncomfortable as the lead speaker for the occasion, I stood to introduce the motion. My strength was my voice, which conveyed weight, even if it shook nervously. Mburu winked at me from the gathered group as if to say that I was doing fine. "Last week," I said, "this association decided to rename this building the Fidel Castro House. Whether or not I personally admire the man is of no consequence. Given the climate we find ourselves in and as guests of a nation so opposed to the man, I move that we vote to annul that vote. Second, I move that we vote to leave the ISA house unnamed until such time as a mutually acceptable name can be found for it. Finally, I move that we vote to apologise to The University for not going through the proper channels in taking the vote in the first place and for later engaging in acts inconsistent with civility."

William Redford couldn't have echoed himself better.

The ISA president objected: "That is just ridiculous! This is a sad apology for the system. Who are you afraid of, man? These are descendents of pimps and prostitutes who've been screwing us over again and again?"

One American student attending the meeting as an observer objected, "As an American I take offense to that."

"Who gives a damn what you think?"

"Come on!" Jose said. "There is no need for this kind of talk. We have enough students here to take a vote, so why don't we? The ISA doesn't belong to any one person. It belongs to all of us. Let's vote."

And we did. On the first matter: voted to annul the name change. On the second matter: voted to leave the building unnamed until a mutually acceptable name could be found. But it appeared that the ISA couldn't go down completely on its knees. We lost the vote for the ISA to apologise.

The next day I was summoned to the president's office. As before, he was furious. Also present were William Redford and Yannis. "What is this? I want an apology and I want it immediately. This can't stand."

"Sir," I said. "We have annulled the vote to change the name of the International Students House to Fidel Castro House, but the vote for an apology was defeated."

"Then," he turned to the president of the ISA and said, "You will have to deliver the apology."

"Absolutely not. This was a collective decision. I have no authority to apologise on behalf of the body."

"You will write a letter to the college newspaper and sign it in your name and as president of the International Students Association. Apologise, you will."

"I will do no such thing."

"Need I remind you that you are here at the pleasure of The University? Need I remind you that The University heavily subsidises your tuition?"

"Is this a threat?"

"I want to see a copy of the apology on my desk by tomorrow afternoon."

We left the meeting with the ISA president still defiant. Yannis wouldn't do it, he said. I'm not sure why I was summoned – perhaps to bear witness to his humiliation? As an example to me? I resented this so much that I was beginning to lose my dislike of Yannis. The next morning all international students got a letter from the ISA president indicating his resignation. The following day his letter appeared in the college newspaper. It was short and signed in his capacity as Former ISA President:

> About a week ago, as president of the International Students Association, I led a movement to rename the Brewer House the Fidel Castro House. After careful consideration, I now realise that said action was taken in haste. I apologise to The University and the American people for that action. I now fully support the most recent decision by the International Students Association to annul that vote. Also on that night, there were some acts on the lawn of The University president's residence. As president of the ISA at the time, I take full responsibility for those acts. I now realise that these acts were improper. I deeply regret them and apologise to all concerned parties.

I knew that despite his fervour, Yannis too had had to bargain his pride, barter it for self-preservation. Days later, against my objections, I was elected president of the ISA. It was a humiliating victory, a badge I wore in memory of my betrayal to *self*. I knew the ISA would never be the same. I died a little. The University had moved a piece on the chessboard and I had no immediate response. It was as if the pawns were moving, the bishops and knights too and I was handicapped, struggling to avoid getting checked. The voice reached me clear and concise like a poignant sermon: Check. But the temporary escape must be there, waiting to be seized. Not yet Checkmate.

It seemed in a way a generous compromise for The University to accept an apology for the cross burning without seeking out the perpetrators and punishing them. It was an act for which The University could impose dismissal. It wouldn't be too difficult to find those involved. But was the president ready for that? Could he stand to dismiss these students, who would represent a broad cross section of the ISA community, for an act borrowed so directly from the history of a nation that still reeled from a raw and painful legacy? A burning cross. Would too much attention to the matter not tear open the thin tissue covering unhealed wounds? A less tactful person might have berated William Redford for devising the strategy that focused on an apology for those "acts" rather than seeking dismissal. But the president was grateful to the ISA adviser. In his view, the ISA adviser had performed a miracle of sorts. Despite calls from *The University Review* for firmer action, the larger campus community seemed content with the outcome. It seems sometimes there's a willingness to move on with an *imperfect* outcome than seek a *perfect* one that could blow open discomforting matters.

So when Professor Redford was named Dean of Students, we all knew he had worked for it. He had saved himself for it, his dream job. I first learned of it when his picture appeared in the college newspaper with the headlines announcing his appointment. I didn't know what to think and therefore feel about him. Was he the welcoming hand that invited me to his home when I first arrived, when we both tried to melt away the distance? Or was he the stern grip holding the disguised knife, compelling me to do his bidding? I forced myself to dismiss him, but he wouldn't reciprocate. He called to invite me to his house for a party to celebrate the occasion. I'm not sure why I didn't find an excuse not to go. Could it be the new fear of him that I'd developed? Having accepted, I went. The bridge over the creek leading to his house squeaked even louder, worsening the fear I'd plunge into it. I hated myself for being so cowardly, but it was what it was. Moreover, John Kennedy had just been assassinated in Dallas. The death of this dashing leader seemed to affect me in a negative way – as it affected Ed and Phoebe. Somehow, my simple fear of the precarious bridge seemed to pale when compared with the gravity of the young leader's death and by this comparison, gave me strength to believe I could traverse the little obstacles ahead of me.

I was one of only two students present: the other was Yannis. That seemed so strange to me. Why would Yannis accept this invitation from a man who'd worked to humiliate him? Was his reason identical to mine? I was determined to find out. I smiled and said generalised nothings to the professors who'd gathered there, just the usual *I'm fine, thanks; Classes are going well,* etc. They all seemed to be leaning closer to me, as if I wasn't talking loud enough. I heard again and again, "Could you speak louder?" I forced my way to Yannis, who had ignored me ever since the incident. I understood. How could I blame him after what I'd done? In fact, I admired him for it and my dislike was inconsequential, dissipated under the common onslaught we both faced. Like me, he had succumbed under the weight of the threat over him. He would be graduating in the spring. He had a lot at stake. But he need not compromise the ensuing anger: he need not talk to me. I asked him why he was there.

He was uncomfortable. "He asked me to come."

"But after all that's happened, I wouldn't expect that you'd accept."

"And why not? You are here, aren't you?"

"Yes, but I'm different. I mean . . . "

"Listen. We both know we don't control our destiny as long as we are here."

"Come on, Yannis. You don't mean that, do you?"

"No, *you* come on. You of all people should understand that, going behind our backs and orchestrating that *coup* with the president and Redford."

"Is that what you think?"

"That's what I know."

I was losing respect for Yannis. Instead of dislike, something like pity for him was seizing me. He appeared so defeated. I could understand that, but this angry apathy was something else. This was not what I'd expected, this defiant man, now so passive. I hated him. He seemed to read my mind when he said so profoundly, "Don't hate yourself so much." Say what? I hating myself? Or I, hating Yannis? Or Yannis hating me? Or a cycle wherein hater and hated was irrelevant so long as there was hate. Who hated whom? Or rather, who pitied whom?

I would have challenged Yannis, but William Redford walked to us and said, "My two most favourite students. What are you doing all by yourselves? Come on and mingle. Don't be shy." He seemed the happiest man. But who wouldn't?

And then two weeks later I saw him walking home from his office. He looked tense, his head bowed, his shoulders hunched, his hands behind him: almost as he'd looked the day he recruited me to crusade against the name change of the International Students Association's house, only this time the defeat seemed complete. The new job couldn't be that challenging. He stopped and looked at me. He appeared to have been crying and to want to cry. His attempt to smile failed. He came closer and put a hand on my shoulder. "How are you keeping?"

"Well, sir," I said, knowing that something was tragically wrong.

"That's good," he said. "You never stop by the house anymore. Winnie has been asking to see you. I think she'd love it if you stopped by the house."

"I will," I said without intending to do so.

"Why don't you come over tonight?"

"Tonight? I..."

"Please, Jojo."

I couldn't understand the professor's plea, but it was so earnest I couldn't reject it.

I was confused. The professor's haunting demeanor, the request made on the precipice of tears... What did it imply? I had a foreboding when I arrived at his home that night. It was an ordinary night: moon, some stars and gentle wind. The bridge over the creek seemed not to squeak as much and my fear of plunging decreased.

William Redford opened the door and let me in. The room held a profound quiet, the lights dimmed so that shadows seemed to creep everywhere. In the sofa sat Winnie Redford. One look and I knew something was wrong with her. Her vitality seemed to have lost significant lustre, nor did she give the same rambunctious greeting that so effortlessly oozed from her previously. "Jojo," she said. "It's so nice to see you again." It was awkward, her voice so thin. Several minutes later she told me she was dying from cancer. She said it without emotion. Either she was resigned to it, I thought, or she'd constructed a façade. "The doctor says I have no more than a month to live." My foreboding had warned me and so I wasn't as surprised as I might have been.

What fuddled me, though, was why she told me. Why me? I couldn't understand the burden they'd decided to place on me, to live with the knowledge that she was going to die. How was I expected to react? I stood there, speechless. Winnie Redford came to me and hugged me. "I've been asking William about you, Jojo. You have something special, you know that? Don't ever lose it. I know it's unfair to you to have to tell you this now, but I want to take the opportunity. You are a good person. William told me how you helped him with the president when the matter about the international students and Fidel Castro came up. He was so proud that you would go to such lengths to help him. You are a good person, Jojo."

Still, the awkwardness I discerned abided even after I left the Redford's that night. I had spent about an hour with them. Winnie Redford showed me photos of herself as a child, as a student (and age had done much to neutralise her youthful beauty), her wedding to William, vacations in England and Germany, photos aboard a cruise ship, smiling and holding on to William. I saw photos of her brother, a scientist who worked with NASA and her sister, an accountant with a major corporation in Dallas. She showed me photos of their families...It was as if she had decided to introduce her life to me and all that came with it.

There seemed no answer to my question: Why me? Her explanation seemed too lame, even spurious. Or was it possible that I had somehow misjudged William Redford's intentions? A kindness that saw itself reflected by others and therefore demanded reciprocity? What kind of confusion was this? I resolved to go back. I couldn't let such confusion continue to torment me. It was strange how so closely drawn I suddenly felt to Winnie Redford and despite my intentions, her husband. Or perhaps I was simply seeing him through her and he was in fact the disguised monster that I'd judged him to be when he sent me on that shameful errand in his quest to become Dean of Students. Because I needed resolution, I went back the next night. Standing outside, I heard strange voices from the room. Professor Redford opened the door and fell – literally fell – into my arms. Winnie Redford had died that afternoon. I posed no further questions to myself, concerned that trying to fathom why they chose me would be as fruitless as seeking the reason for life itself.

The death of Winnie Redford impacted me inexplicably, except for the lame reason that it was the first death I'd experienced in America. As if a relative had died, I couldn't let her death be, especially after I saw Professor Redford walking the campus a few weeks later. The world seemed to have ended for him; a man I'd admired at the beginning, felt betrayed by (at which time my feeling towards him wavered between ambiguous and dislike) and then felt somewhat sympathetic to when his wife died. He'd been reserved even before Winnie's death, but after she died, he hardly spoke. He walked the campus quietly, discharged his duties efficiently but without much passion and seemed to be marking time towards his own death. To me, that was the saddest succumbing. I wanted to shake him out of his prolonged reverie, tell him to live because life had to be lived. But what standing did I have? What basis did I (in my youth, eyeing a life yet to be lived) have to advise a man whose skin seemed to hang loose on him from a life lived and aged? The man seemed to have died. That I recognised this living death of his resurfaced my own unshakable link to the situation. William Redford had never been talkative or ebullient; therefore, his recoil from his surroundings wasn't ostentatious. This was a subtle withdrawal that only careful scrutiny would betray: the remnants of redness left in the eyes, the slight furrow of strain on the forehead, the ever so slight sinking of the cheeks and above all, the melancholy that would not betray itself except through the empathy of the observer.

The melancholy infected me. Ed was flummoxed. "The guy used you," he said. "How can you feel sorry for him?" I wished there were easy answers that silence or sadness could offer, for I had plenty of both. The almost desperate wish by Ed to cheer my mood took the form of partying. He prodded me against my resistance to go to Frat Row with him. I'd not really been much of a drinker, but with so much free beer, I realised my consumption was increasing. I made several efforts (rather lame) to bed a woman. I needed some solace for my ego, something to reassure me of my worth, to demonstrate to me that life offered more than death and depression. I failed repeatedly. I was beginning to doubt myself.

"You want a woman, get the fat ones," Mburu advised. "These white guys don't like them. But me, I don't care. In fact, I like some steak on my women."

"I don't like fat women."

"You think you can get the thin white chicks? Man, there's too much competition for that."

But Mburu's advice put me in a quandary. Clearly, he preferred, or thought he had to pursue, voluptuous women. Conversely, Ed preferred them thin, much too thin for my tastes. He'd fallen in love (actually lust) with one of our mates: Liddy. But, oh my, oh my, she was way too flat. "She has no behind," I remarked.

"Man, her ass is so cute. What're you talking about?"

And to my surprise, he won the argument with the rest of our dorm mates: Liddy was *hot*, they said. I wanted to prove that general view wrong, but it was like forcing fish to sunbathe. Notwithstanding this daunting task, I was confident. If words failed, what better way to prove my point than by comparison? I began a careful study of the female behind. I followed and studied the flat ones in motion – sure, there was an elegance in the fluvial ease of movement, but was that enough? I studied them at standstill as well, when they had come to rest. I made Ed go to school with me on this one. That was when I discovered that my notion of a well rounded behind was considered a *fat ass in the US*.

What? Did Joan, for example, have a fat ass? "Yes!" Ed exclaimed. I was flabbergasted. And then when Ed broadcast my view of Joan, the entire dorm confirmed his view once again: Joan had a fat butt. I crushed a bit under the onslaught. Call it dissonance of sorts, cognitive or emotional or optical. I questioned my tastes. Only one person could rescue me from the abyss of utter self-doubt, but even she now was a memory, even if a robust one. I recalled Marjorie, the rounded flesh behind her that I was so proud of, and she was even more endowed there than Joan. So she had a fat ass too? Slowly, after this crisis of view and taste, I began to conquer my lust for Joan. It was a convenient way of ridding myself of the lust that had reigned: She was a fat ass, after all. So many people couldn't be wrong. What had I seen in her? I wrote several letters to Marjorie as if to kill the threat posed by the crisis. The contradiction wasn't lost on me. I said to myself that even if Marjorie were a fat ass, my love for her would transcend such a blemish in any case. But my eyes and my mind's eyes would be bullied into submission by the images I was constantly told were better until I learned to prefer that version of beauty and I began to admire flatter behinds, too. Unlike Mburu or Dwayne (who after all, had Tanya who was as well endowed as Joan).

While I was indulging myself thus, Professor Redford would invite me to his home from time to time. He even organised parties for selected faculty and students. He had regained a bit of his former self, but I knew he would never recover it completely. That was now self-evident: the smile that failed to mask the sadness, the deepened quietness that bespoke pain rather than mere introspection. And his periodic invitations helped me, as Ed insisted we frequent parties so he could point out cute behinds to me. Seeing William Redford in the company of others signalled to me he would go on, that he could serve his sentence with dignity. After all, that was all anyone could ask of him. The rest was no one else's business.

And then that Thanksgiving, Ed took me home to Somerville. "You can't stay here all by yourself," he said. All Ed wanted to talk about on the trip to Somerville was *doing* Liddy. We spent that Thursday helping his parents clean the house for the company at dinner: an uncle and his three teenage children, one of whom ignored me and two of whom pestered me with questions about Africa. Much as I explained that Africa was a continent, most of which I'd not visited, I couldn't get them to make their questions specific to Ghana.

Then back to school and frat parties . . . and a week later, Ed got his wish: Liddy slept with him. I laboured in the bedroom, tortured by their grunts and moans in the living room. And my penis rose stiff against the sheets, my imagination roaming to Marjorie and Phoebe in lustful wishes that remained unreleased. In my unfulfilled lustfulness, I compared the behinds of the two women in my mind. Forget what anybody else said, I loved Marjorie, even if she had a fat ass. My attraction to Phoebe was something else. Initially, it was an attraction despite her flat behind, but now that I had learned to admire behinds like hers, the attraction was even stronger.

Ed was so jubilant the next day. "She made me work so hard for that," he said. I expected they'd stay together. "No way," said Ed. After Liddy, the floodgates seemed to open for Ed. He joined the sexual revolution, bedding one woman after another, while I continued to have no luck. When I complained to Dwayne, he said it was my fault. "I set you up with Joan and you messed it up." But I was way beyond Joan's fat ass. I had to make love to Marjorie. In my dreams and reveries, I recalled every moment we'd spent together, all intimate and non-intimate ones. It was a source of sustenance in the dry parches of sexual starvation. It wasn't by choice, but I ratified my celibacy by affirming that it was for Marjorie's sake.

And then came Norah Turner.

Eight

My first winter had passed slowly like a lingering distasteful odour: the punishing cold, the long times spent indoors, bouts with flu, the females who neighboured me but gave me no sex. I hadn't gone home that Christmas because I couldn't afford it. I was reluctant to ask Uncle Kusi to fund the trip, though I knew he'd have obliged me. It had been a dreadful period without Marjorie, thoughts of her, her warmth, now stifled cold by distance. I stared time and again at her pictures, a lame substitute for her physical presence. I simply *survived* and *went* to school. I had little choice, if any. Young and still believing anything possible, although expectations were sometimes tempered, my thoughts about an alluring future would roam wild and sometimes unchecked. Ordering pizza on Saturday nights, huddling with a few friends watching a movie on television, studying or chatting about women and politics, I survived and went to school. Walking through the snow and wondering what a man from Ghana was doing in these parts, building a sculpture in the snow and almost freezing, I maintained my sanity. Going to work and classes and then work, earning meagre wages and clenching my teeth when I used some on beer, I looked forward to better days.

And then the spring emerged with its torrent of hormones; the campus dotted with women with long, slender, shaven legs (and of course, some bandy ones as well) donning shorts shorter than skirts. I was in high drive for sexual release, perhaps even desperate for it. I was in that heightened state when I went to the library to check out a book for a history class. The clerk at the checkout desk took the book, looked up and asked, "Do you have your ID?" I gave it to her. "Jojo Badu. Never heard that one before."

I paid her heightened attention. "It's Ghanaian. You won't see many names like that around here."

"Ghanaian. That's African, right?"

"Yes."

"That's pretty cool. I'd love to go to Africa sometime."

"You will love it."

"I bet." She gave me back the book and ID. "See you around."

"What's your name?"

"Norah Turner."

A pleasant encounter I ignored after I left the library. I could ill afford the torment of expectations that would go unfulfilled. But a week later I saw her in The University Park in a bikini, reading a book and tanning. Out of the many leggy women sunbathing, I isolated and stared at her half-nudity, perhaps a little too emboldened by the pleasant memory of our meeting at the library. "Jojo, right?"

"You remember my name."

"Sure, I remember. What're you up to?"

"I was going back to the dorm."

"Yeah? And when you get back to the dorm, what are you going to do. Study? Nap?"

"I will study for a while, I suppose."

"Is that all you Africans do, study?"

"How many Africans do you know?"

She beamed, inviting me into her smile. Was that smile for seduction or mere friendship? I craved for the former as she said, "One."

"Just one?"

I stood there a full five minutes, talking; she, propping her head on her elbows, squinting at me. I fought to keep my gaze on her face (green eyes, long lashes, thin lips) but the invitation was too tempting and the allure drew my attention to the rest of her, her flat belly, slim arms and long legs. She wasn't unusual – many like her lay on the green of The University Park. Still, she was unusual, for she was getting to know me. But I refused to give the experience wings to take flight. Not yet. Eight days later, though, I ran into her in a fraternity. After a long bout of studying, I'd reluctantly followed Ed to the Kappa Sigma Kappa frat, into a tee-shirted and jeans-wearing tangle of bodies talking amid the incessant sipping of beer and hopping to loud rock and roll – an illustration of dancing without rhythm.

"Kind of boring up here," Ed said.

I disagreed silently. Even if devoid of the grace of rhythm, the mere sight of such physical force, women dancing by leaping up into the air, their loose body parts shaking abundantly, heads swaying almost unchecked... that was a sexually charged sight that held my attention. But to see without sharing was torment. "Yes, do you want to get out of here then?" I said.

"Let's go get some beer in the basement. Never say no to free beer."

The basement was its usual spectacle. It seemed beer had been spilled deliberately on the floor so we could almost feel the sticky wetness under our feet. The smell was stale and annoying, but not abhorrent yet. As we drank, I noticed Norah walk in with a friend. Norah's red hair flamed in the relative dimness of the fraternity basement. A third experience of her presence . . . Would this do it?

"Here's my friend Laura," she said. I introduced Ed. As Laura and Ed started conversing, I had to make conversation with Norah, a generally welcome situation that was nonetheless stifled with nervous charge. We spoke generally, of schoolwork and courses, and then she asked, as she pulled slowly on her hair, "So what do you do for fun?"

"Nothing much, I suppose."

"This is college, Jojo, you've got to have fun. I've got to show you how to have fun. The American way. Like, I mean, what do you do for fun in Africa?"

"There's a lot to do. Films . . . "

"Movies? In Africa?"

"Yes. Why, is that hard to believe?"

"Well, I guess . . . I don't know . . . "

Laura turned to Norah. "We've got to go."

"Remember what I said," Norah intoned to me and then they were gone.

"What did you do to her?" I asked Ed.

"Nothing. Forget her."

"It looked to me like you two were getting along."

"Yeah, she's full of nonsense."

"You messed up. Norah was warming up to me."

"Dream on."

"I'm serious. I think she likes me."

"Then why don't you ask her out?"

"Ask her out?"

"What have you got to lose? She's hot. Ask her out!"

"And if she says no?"

"Then the hell with her."

We saw Phoebe in the distance as we left Frat Row. I hadn't seen her in a long while. Stimulated by the most recent meeting with Norah, I wished for female contact. The unsubstantiated image returned of Phoebe taking off my clothes the night we first met, not something I wanted to relive in her presence. It seemed so silly given that we'd spent time together at the rally. She called after us. "You go to the fraternities?" she asked.

"Went for a few beers," Ed said.

"Don't you see what these fraternities stand for?"

"What's that?"

"Come on Ed, do I need to tell you? This is the height of white male patriarchy, man. No place can be more sexist, racist and xenophobic."

And come to think of it, frequenting fraternities seemed inconsistent with Ed's professed principles and perhaps mine as well.

Ed made a face. "What are you up to anyway?"

"I just came from a meeting. We're trying to organize a protest. You know Manhattan Bank is coming to campus tomorrow to recruit. That bank just wrote some huge loans to South Africa. They're supporting the racist system of South Africa.

We can't not do nothing about that, you know. Plus, we'll be protesting the draft as well. You want to join us?"

"Sounds great," Ed said. "How come I didn't know about this?

"We just found out. Plus you're not going to find out by horsing around on Frat Row."

"We weren't horsing around."

"You're coming, Jojo?" I felt naked before her, but she seemed so comfortable. *Am I coming, Phoebe*? I couldn't. Or rather wouldn't. The draft was a bit remote from me, given that all the young men I knew at the time had managed to gain deferment from the war, but I knew the potential of being called one day was real and better to prevent than to wait for it to happen and then try to cure. I remembered Ed's various complaints that he couldn't see how he could find himself serving in a war he didn't believe in. I wasn't sure, though, if his conscientious objection would suffice if the need to find able-bodied men caught up with him. Dwayne almost echoed Mohammed Ali's later statement that no Vietcong ever called him nigger when he said to me, "This isn't my war. Why fight for so-called freedom when my own people are second-class citizens right here in their country of birth?" I knew these were important matters, of life, death and conscience, but I wondered if I could risk any open defiance after the International Students Association incident? Was I not under a microscope? What would William Redford do if he knew I was engaged in an event so clearly political? Or did it even matter? Would The University view a protest as an open act of defiance or a privileged student's noblesse oblige? Would they see it as an important extension of intellectual dialogue or an empty-headed expression of youthful foolishness?

"I will be there," I lied. Phoebe smiled at me. I confessed to Ed that I didn't intend to go. He was aghast at my deception and tried to convince me otherwise. I resisted. Why was he so interested anyway? I asked him. Why did he, despite his obviously privileged background, seem drawn to the protests of the time. That's when he took me with him to his high school years.

Born in 1945, by the time Ed was in high school the effects of The Great Depression were receding, the country was rebuilding on the pungent carcass of World War II, opportunities were opening afresh and his parents were accumulating wealth. Ed was privileged in that he'd not lived through either of those shaping events. They were events read about on the dead pages of books, seen on the lame reels of motion and still pictures, and heard on audiotapes. He saw possibilities within his privilege, except they were possibilities mired in boredom: for him it meant playing piano (which his parents had made him learn to play), school, homework, football practice and games, time out with his friends, catching a movie here and there and going to parties that seemed too sanitised (even with the drinking and sex), as well as spending stale time with the obligatory girlfriend approved by his parents. For him, such boredom offered by wealth was a counterfeit of life and had to yield to something different.

He needed a new crowd. Purposefully, he sought the rebellious of those among his peers, stirred on by the constant replaying of James Dean and Marlon Brando movies, particularly *Rebel Without a Cause*. The group he found in the fringe crowd of high school smoked pot and broke rules. Privileged, yes, but rebellious. It was during this time that he first felt alienated from his parents. They were enmeshed too deeply in their daily lives of acquiring wealth to acquire the *consciousness* that Ed was beginning to seek, the internal battle, the difficulty of reconciling this idyllic world with the threat and fear of possible nuclear obliteration. There had to be something more than what was promised by the *establishment* he knew, something deeper and more fulfilling. He sought deeper into the other world he didn't know. He befriended black kids. He discovered the music of Chuck Berry, Little Richard and Fat's Domino. No matter if it was Negro/Nigger music. It had resonance with him. Even if it didn't erase the itch inside him, it scratched it.

In search of options, Ed read more on Marxism. It appealed to him, but it seemed so largely handicapped by the totalitarianism of the Soviet Union, which to him was Marxism in practice. He found no exit, yet the capitalism he enjoyed seemed too *status quo* for his taste. He knew no way to change it, though, so he rebelled as his peers did: he changed his appearance; he dumped his girlfriend. She seemed too proper, too lacking in ambition, too bereft of *consciousness*. And so, wherever a protest, there he found himself, still searching – a rebel seeking his cause and therefore malleable.

I felt I understood Ed better after this brief autobiographical sketch, but it wasn't he that interested me at the time. I laboured over the prospect of a more immediate need, an absorbing presence. But how would Norah react if I propositioned her? With so many factors (such as race and culture) shrouding the possibilities that might be, would she seek shelter in that shroud, or would she risk the unknown, the risqué, the venturous? But was I getting ahead of myself? All I needed to do was ask for a date. I called Mburu. "You've got to try it once," he said, as though it was a mere intrigue; a hunger once fed, forever satisfied. But there was more than that. I actually liked her. And I knew the danger of mixing experimentation with emotion. And then there was Marjorie, hanging in memory.

Five days after I spoke with Mburu, I went to the hallway in my dorm and called Norah from the pay phone. With an infirm voice, I asked, "Do you want to have dinner on Friday?"

"Friday? Oh yes, that'd be great."

And that was the beginning, but it would meander towards an end, an end not easily defined, not smoothly demarcated. The first date was cordial, but uneventful, especially judged against spending my meagre earnings on an expensive meal. I learned a little more about her. Her father was an architect; her mother, an engineer. She was born and raised in Saint Louis, Missouri, played hockey in high school and ran track. But she had a way of extending subjects, digging into nuances and describing them and extending our conversation beyond its sparse subject matters. Plus she had an arsenal of questions, mostly directed at unearthing the mystery that was Africa. "I'd love to do a safari sometime, you know, see all the animals." Animals. Animals. Animals. I was disappointed but forgave her.

After dinner, I wanted to walk her to her dorm, but she said she needed to pick up some groceries. "Thanks for dinner," she said as if to signal she had no additional use for me. Was this Joan in repeat? (Except Norah had no fat ass by any means.) This was the cutest of the cutest: flat and firm. She reached out with a hand and stroked my cheek and I liked the redolence of her perfume. Then she walked away.

In the later night, reliving the earlier one, my memory remoulded her every word, her every act into a soothing stream of nocturnal joy. I called her the next night to ask if she'd like to see a movie. Yes, she said. So we saw a movie that Saturday. I was quiet for the most part, wondering what the *terra incognita* held, as I sat tensely beside her. We walked out into the dark night of spring. "What do you want to do?" she asked. "It's still early, don't you think? I think we should do something." I hesitated. "I tell you what," she said, "let's go back to my room. We've never really talked, you and I. I want to know more about you, you know what I mean? I feel like you're a friend now, but it's like I don't really know who you are. What do you think?"

"I think it's a good idea."

She had a single room, furnished with a couch, a television, phone and radio. "It's a very nice room," I said. It was a paraphrased line I'd picked up from some movie.

"It's okay," she said, shrugging. We talked the bulk of the night, me sitting on the carpeted floor, she sitting on her bed. She let me more into her world of high school, the boys she dated, her parents, her brother and her three sisters. "I'm getting kind of hungry again," she said, against the train of conversation.

"So am I."

"Well, I don't have anything to eat, although I guess we could order something. But I'm not that hungry."

"I don't know if we can find a place still opened at this time."

"Wait, I have a couple of apples."

She opened her refrigerator and retrieved a pair of apples and held both in her hands for a while, caressing them as if removing some blemish, the pair of apples that looked as soft as flesh and ruby red. *No. No. Not this fruit*. Did she realise what she was doing, the obvious implications? She put one on top of the refrigerator and bit a chunk of the other. "Here," she said, offering it to me. I too took it and bit a chunk. I stuck my tongue into it, rolling it around and thrusting it back and forth, finding seeds and licking on them. It yielded to my long probe and I reached deeper until its juices wet my lips. I withdrew to breathe for a moment and then I pushed back in. That way we took turns eating the first apple.

"Pretty good, huh?" she asked.

"Yes."

"Here, let's eat the other one."

She gave it to me. I bit into it and gave it to her. We finished the second apple, too.

Then she asked, "Do you have a girlfriend at home?"

Where was this leading? My heart tapped my chest increasingly forcefully.

"Not really." *Marjorie, I'm so sorry.*

"And you're not dating anyone here?"

"No." Then shyly I added, "Except you." I had done my part of the gamble.

Shyly she asked, "Ever slept with an American woman?"

Shyly I said, "No."

That was when it happened. The shyness was the catalyst, the attraction masked in the fear of overt boldness, at the same time as it refused to pass without reward. It was as if we both knew by instinct we'd reached the bifurcating road, when the night's tension would be consummated (damn the consequences) or let die in a whimper (damn the consequences as well). And so our reaching for each other, rubbing, exchanging of fluids, the performance, all had as a backdrop the choice of one damnation over the other. Either way, we both knew there might be regret as much as there might be satisfaction and experience. But in that short moment when the feared or welcome aftermath was subverted on the alter of pleasurable congress, we chose to speak with that unified voice, merging the conclusions of the two options we'd faced before the act that spoke with one voice: damn the consequences – an affirmation and a negation coexisting without rancour; yes, damn the consequences ringing hollow in the midstream of consummation. Tasted of the forbidden fruit, now self-aware. Marked.

...Now the decision to tell Marjorie...I'd not written her since I started dating Norah, who affected me as an earthquake, with a shudder when we were together and an aftershock when we were separated. Marjorie had written twice. I could have pretended I still had her front and centre of my thoughts, but I didn't want to be that selfish. And what if Norah found out? The latter risk, I didn't want to bear. I wrote Marjorie a very terse letter. There was no suitable explanation. I simply informed her that it was time to break up. She wrote twice after that asking me to reconsider, to remember our commingled blood. I didn't reply. She wrote three times after that. I never replied to any of them.

And so the first spring at The University was a script from a fantastic fictional romance. The relationship with Norah moved forward. We went to the cafeteria often, went to the library together and studied together (thereby inviting gossip). I knew it, but there was so much pleasure to be drawn that the talk and chatter fell against the oblivious shelter we offered each other. It was Dwayne who tampered with this seemingly impenetrable halo of romance: "Brother, what're you doing with that white chick?"

"I am dating her." An answer bold and defiant, with which I meant to project my irritation.

Shaking his head, Dwayne asked, "Are you free for lunch?"

We sat across from each other. "I'm telling you, man, it ain't worth it. Why don't you want one of your own?"

"Why does it bother you so much?"

"My brother," Dwayne said, "Listen to me. I'll only say this once. When these white chicks see you, especially when they're drunk, all they see is one big dick. If you only want to be seen as a sex object, that's up to you. I guess if you're looking for just fun, that's okay, but then you've got to move on."

I heard. But how deeply could I hear? I'd have wanted to open up the experience with Norah to Dwayne, the pages inscribed with pleasures that only the participants could truly know, although even an observer might notice its sweetness. But I refrained from that frontal approach. "So what do you want me to do?"

"Find yourself a black woman."

"But I can't do that." Hell, where had Joan left me?

"Listen, Jojo. Listen good. Do you know what you're doing when you walk across campus with that woman? Do you? You're insulting every black woman on campus. You hear me? You're saying they're not good for you. You're telling your own mother, your own sisters, that they ain't worth what a white woman's worth."

I'd heard that before. Could Dwayne not do better than echo this cliché? Could we not simply love for love's sake? Ought anyone to read other meanings when we didn't? Or were we being naïve? Were our actions inextricably intertwined with external factors that defined us? "It has nothing to do with that," I said, looking for a voice amid these myriad thoughts, but unable to articulate the questions that whirled through my mind. That would be too exhausting.

"It's got everything to do with that. Hell, brother, I gave you a black woman and you reject her for this?"

"Come on Dwayne, you know it just didn't work out with Joan." She didn't like me, I should have said.

"Yeah, whatever. Be careful, brother."

His caution seemed to suck the waters right out of me, out of my throat. Although Dwayne's words resounded afterwards, Norah made them ricochet ineffectually. Unlike the clichés of words, she knew how to find the clichés of romance. On a moonlit night, while I observed the light wash over her face, she asked, "Tell me how you love me." It was the first mention of love between us. I looked at her anew and knew I had to find the words and turn them in at once gently but forcefully: a massive wave that offers a slow breeze.

"It is like a calm storm." This terse response seemed all she needed. She pondered it a while and grinned as if swept into an envelope of passion. "I too love you like a calm storm," she echoed. Norah hugged me tightly, a little too tightly and I gasped. Although Dwayne's caution sat at the back of my mind, I had little room to let it fester.

Then time passed and grew on us its rust but, more importantly, its experience. Slowly spring yielded. The rain that replaced snow in April formed a wet segue to the month of May. Even when it didn't fall, the sky was often pregnant with rain. May too came to a close and the heat of June warmed up towards the furnace of July. Norah and I walked out of the library into the heat. Our oblivion had started to crack. More and more, I noticed the sneer on a face while we walked by, the puzzled stare as though Norah and I were freaks, even the hostile glances, all of which I'd seen before but ignored. In our earlier days together, the passion was too hot to suffer these gestures, but in the ebbed heat, when lust plateaus, I became vulnerable. I was particularly perplexed when on the way home one night with her after a movie in the town, I heard someone yell from a passing car: "Have you been black all your life?" We both pretended we hadn't heard, but it was a futile effort of bravery, at least for me. She put out her hand into mine, perhaps a gesture of physical support where words wouldn't help. I was uncomfortable. Pretending I needed to cough, I pulled my hand from hers to stifle the forced cough and returned the hand to my pocket. Did she notice this act of retreat? "You want to get something to eat?" she asked.

"I have to meet Ed to go over some stuff." A lie with a history. A history with a story. A story with bottomless riddles. Riddles seemingly mired in fathomless contortions.

"What kind of stuff?"

"Guy stuff."

"All right. Call me later if you want to do dinner."

I walked away from my source of discomfort, even though her company was enjoyable . . . if ever there was a paradox . . . More and more I wished to relegate our times together to closed places: the dorm and our rooms. How do you escape the stare as hard as anger that seems to penetrate bones? How do you manage that sneer you know contains a million words unspoken? I didn't want to lose her and still I desired somehow to be free of her company. These were perplexing matters to which no answers surfaced. I didn't call Norah for dinner. In fact, it was as if I found myself as a part of her, yet needed to find myself by negating her. I went to my room and ordered pizza and ate alone. The cowardliness gnawed at my ego. And yet I didn't call her the next day either. She called instead. We spoke briefly without planning to meet.

I continued to think of her without knowing what to do. The next day, I picked up a copy of *The University Review*. An article on multiculturalism stared at me from the front page. It lambasted it as "a failed attempt to force ludicrous notions of a multicultural campus at the expense of scholarship." It read in part:

> It makes absolutely no sense that the bulk of those who champion so called diversity are the very ones who promote segregation. The Afro-American House is a case in point. Can you imagine if The University were to sanction an Anglo-Saxon House? The uproar would be immediate and loud. Yet The University welcomes black self-segregation for a people whose future success in the nation depends on their ability to integrate into the larger society. Last I checked, that larger society was not black. This, after all, is not Africa. If the attitude of Negro students for the privilege of admission to The University is self-segregation, then perhaps it is time for The University to reevaluate its criteria for admission. How far will Afro-Americans carry such segregation? Will they also refuse to integrate into the civilised community at large? Will they be

ready to return then to the dark crevices of civilization, that massive failure of nature's experiment called Africa?"

Something died inside me when I read the article, especially when I saw that John wrote it. I rushed to see John, intending to berate him for the article. But before I could speak, he asked, "So, how's Norah?"

"She's fine."

"So you think you'll be together a while?"

"Why do you ask?"

John's face flushed. "Nothing," he said. "Just making talk."

There was an uncomfortable nervousness about him. "Talk to me," I implored.

"Don't you feel like being with your own kind? I mean, don't get me wrong. Whatever two people decide to do is their own business, but doesn't this business get funny? Hey, I don't want you to take offense."

Offended? Not then, to be truthful. I just had to yield a little bit of myself, subrogate it to that emotion which suppresses difficult thoughts and reactions – the nature of the monster after all was to seize a little bit of the self and suppress it with the inconspicuous but persistent crawl of realities. I was a notch wiser. I remembered a conversation with Mburu: "Be careful, my brother, this is their greatest treasure. You are invoking all kinds of psychosexual complexes each time you walk with Norah across campus."

So what was I to do? Were John, Dwayne and Mburu saying the same thing in different words? What about Ed? "You think I should break up with Norah?"

"Are you crazy? You two are so good together."

"Yes, but she's white."

"Are you some raving racist or something? What does that have to do with anything?"

"You don't understand, Ed. Have you ever been with a black woman?"

"No, but it wouldn't be a problem for me if I fell in love with one."

"It takes love? You've never seen one you liked?"

"Man, what's this? Some kind of interrogation? This isn't fair, you know."

I watched Ed's face flush red, as if my question had lit a fire of discomfort. I didn't push him. I would need to consult the most important person whose honest opinions I'd taken for granted so far: myself. It was one thing to move with the flow of the wind, its colourless breeze; it was another thing to stop once in a while and take heed of the trees and the rivers along the way, the hard barks, the broken bridges over heated rivers. In the meantime, though, I wanted to know John's story. What were the crevices hidden behind the façade? I began probing, trying to discover a little of his background.

John was terse, but he told me enough. He was born in Casper, Wyoming in 1943. While his father worked as editor of the leading local newspaper, his mother kept the home. John's crowd was exclusively white: all the way through high school. When the civil rights movement was reported in the news, his father would throw his hands in the air and say, "Why can't the Negroes stay to themselves?" It was a question that needed no elaboration and went unchallenged by John's mother, who treated her husband's every word as if it was divinely inspired. The son wouldn't parse the words either. After all, his own life was a testimony to the racial apartness his father suggested. "I hate the physical violence," the older man said, "but what kind of world would we live in if we allowed desegregation? We're just different people, blacks and whites and there's no need to change what the good Lord has made." When the US Supreme Court asked for desegregation in the *Brown v. Board of Education* decision in 1954, the older man editorialised in part: "As much as we love our Negro brothers and sisters, it seems to flout the natural order of things to require desegregation of our public schools. What God has ordained, let no man put asunder. Today, the Supreme Court seeks to usurp the Natural Law of God." John, who spent time at his father's office, observed the older man agonise over the wording of the editorial, admiring the effort he put into it. But the older man never used foul language when he referred to the Negroes, at least not in the presence of his family. He never advocated violence against them and never deprecated the race. He just believed they were different, a little inferior with occasional flashes of brilliance and had a culture that would corrupt the white race.

The younger man, therefore, grew up not so much with a hatred of black people, but something resembling mistrust – deeply suspicious of the changes around him, he was as curious as he was fearful that desegregation was somewhat a threat to his race. It was with that view that he entered college. And seeking to follow where his father trod, he joined the staff of the most conservative newspaper off-campus.

I left John's apartment not having accomplished my mission, but somehow his narration seemed to have reduced my anger.

"I knew he's a blatant fascist." Ed said later.

Giving its timing, the article became one more shot at me – and at Norah and me. I was embittered by it, its tone; worse, I was bitter towards Norah. And later still, Dwayne would say to me, "Saw what your friend wrote in *The University Review*?"

"Who says he's my friend?"

"Whatever you say, brother."

I felt their accusatory voices wagging at me; that I was at fault somehow for my association with John. "See what they think of you?" Ed had added. And it seemed as if in spite of my will, I was yielding to something almost sinister and suspicious. I felt I had to question motives, look behind smiles. It was new ground, perhaps dangerous, perhaps robbing me of my happiness, but apparently necessary.

I went to see Norah. "We need to talk, Norah."

"Anything the matter?"

I sat next to her on the bed and let my hand rest on her lap. "We need to talk."

"You already said that."

I couldn't look at her when I said, "There's something not right between us, Norah."

"What do you mean?"

"We've never really discussed it, Norah, but we must. This colour thing."

"What about it? I don't understand."

"Come on. You know what I mean. We have a problem."

"What problem?"

"Be honest, Norah. Be honest. You can't just sit here and pretend. You know I love you, but you're white and I'm black. You're American and I'm African. There's too much dividing us. Every time we step out it's as if we are being observed and judged . . . People staring at us and making remarks. I could go on and on. It's just too hard." She was silent, but her face reddened. I went on, "You can't tell me you don't feel the same pressure."

She swallowed hard. "I do too," she said. "But everybody faces some pressure of some sort once they walk out of their door. Everyone is judged one way or the other. We can work through this."

"Yes? How come you never invite me to meet your friends, even introduce me to them?"

"What a thing to say. I always do."

"This is Jojo. That I've heard you say. But this is my boyfriend? Never."

"Give me time. Plus, everyone knows we're dating, anyway. We don't need to say it to them in their faces."

"Is that right, this pretense? And how much time? It's because I'm black, isn't it? Would you have any reservations if I wasn't? If I were white?"

"You know better than that."

"Norah, you are human. Weak. I am too. I can't blame you. But where does that leave us?"

"Let's take it one step at a time."

"It's not right. If we can't do it the right way, it's not worth doing at all."

She took my hands and squeezed them. "Don't talk like that."

It was now or never, I decided. Because I couldn't muster the courage to yell back at the imprisonment imposed on us, I was about to choose the practical over the bold. "I think we should break up."

She swallowed hard again. She bit her lip gently (not hard enough to draw blood). (Mark the moment? No blood.) "Are you serious?"

"I'm sure you want the same thing, too."

"I've thought about it, but never really thought we'd break up this way."

That was all the verification I needed, support for the belief I was doing it for us both.

"Don't leave," she said as I started for the door.

"I have to. We are just friends from now on."

"Friends? What do you mean friends? If you leave, Jojo, we're through. I can't be just friends."

"You'll change your mind," I said, hoping to run as far as possible. If I stayed any longer, I'd go back and gather her and hold her and it would begin again. I walked out of the room.

Ed would tell me how stupid I was. And I did feel stupid. And extremely pained. Yet I felt relieved, as though I'd unchained myself, reintroduced a waft of fresh air – like a man who emerges from a tunnel into the vastness of the outside. But three times in the night I woke up and went to the phone, pulling together all my will not to call and again hear Norah in her enthusiasm. I saw Dwayne the next day. "What's up, bro?"

"Nothing," I said, rubbing bloodshot eyes.

"Huh? Speak louder, bro, what's wrong?"

"You won't understand."

"Hey, try me."

"I broke up with Norah."

Dwayne didn't laugh, nor even hint joy. "The white girl?"

"Yes."

"I know the feeling, man. It ain't easy to break up with a woman you like, you know. You need plenty of time and space."

Know the feeling? How could Dwayne know? This man who'd taunted me about Norah, who ought to be rejoicing that his wish was fulfilled. How could he know? This man who had Tanya.

"You know, you need to get your mind focused on something, keep it occupied. Like next week, me and a couple of my friends are getting together to protest that stupid article in *The University Review*. You want to join us?"

"I can't do that, Dwayne."

"I understand, brother. You need some time to yourself. Hey, but if you change your mind, let me know. And keep your head up, brother. You're a warrior, a Zulu warrior."

No, Dwayne, I'm Asante and I don't feel like a warrior of any kind.

I ate miserably and went back to the dorm. I mentioned the rally to Ed. "I'm going," he said.

"Really?"

"Yeah. Why, you're not going?"

"I don't think so."

"But why? *The University Review* writes all this nasty stuff and you don't care?"

"This way of doing things is not my style. I don't do too well in such protests."

"As you wish, Jojo. But someone has to stand up to these guys."

And from all accounts, the rally against *The University Review* was a success, drawing over an eighth of the student population in protest. Phoebe came to see me later, hugging me tightly. "Ed told me you broke up with your girlfriend," she said. "She doesn't know what she's lost. Don't worry about it, Jojo. It will pass." She chided me mildly for not coming to the rally. "You've got to get with it, Jojo. Stay focused." Before she left she said, "Hey, if you ever want to talk, call me, okay?" I wanted to talk, but I didn't call her.

The University Review followed the rally with an article upbraiding the "forces against truth and reason". "I hate *The University Review*," Dwayne said to me. "I hate John. He's a racist."

Nine

It was like that, one looking one way and the other looking the other way, not talking, set in ways both old and new. There could be no bridge between the unlinked unless someone built it. But who would lay the first brick of the foundation? Sometimes an extraordinarily farsighted person does. Sometimes, though, the river must overflow, boiling red, before the first brick is laid. The first threat of an overflow was soon to come. It happened on a Saturday night. (Why do those late hours seem to attract such deeds?) Three men set off from their rooms dressed in sweat suits, each holding a plastic bag in which he'd placed his attire for the night's planned deed. A fourth had left earlier to reconnoitre and call the rest to say that the Afro-American House was empty. It was a night carefully chosen because of a ceremony at The University library in honour of WEB DuBois, an event certain to draw the Afro-Am crowd away. The calculated risk appeared to have worked.

The men approached the Afro-Am House cautiously, looking around to ensure they could progress unobserved. It was the end of a drab day unusual for that time of the year (cold temperatures, wind, rain and moody clouds). Their stealth seemed in synch with the weather. Slowly they entered the Afro-Am House and climbed up the stairs to the common room a floor above, checking first to be doubly sure it was indeed empty. Once inside the common room, they retrieved from their plastic bags white makeshift gowns made from bed sheets and then the white hoods with slits for the eyes. They donned their gowns and hoods.

The leader of the group took from his pocket a little white cross – half an arm long – on which was carved a body painted black. But instead of crucifixion, the black figure hung by the neck from the cross. In place of what would have been INRI were inscribed the words "King of the Niggers". The revealed cross seemed to embolden the strength of the group. The leader leaned the cross on the wall, next to the photographs of Malcolm X and Martin Luther King, briefly stalled by what appeared a contradiction. He retrieved a camera and took pictures.

It had been adventurous, perhaps even stupid, given the enormous risk they'd taken, but then a sense of superiority carried its twin of false invincibility. Plus in their minds this was entirely justified when taken in the context of the cross burned earlier on the president's front lawn. Mission impossible seemingly accomplished. But as they readied to leave, they heard sounds of voices and footsteps. How could that be when the WEB DuBois ceremony was scheduled to last at least another hour? They panicked, pushing out of the common room, not thinking to shed the gowns and hoods. They bumped into a group in the hallway as they ran out. The confrontation and fight was inevitable. Outnumbered, the intruders were overpowered and their hoods removed, except one among them who leaped forward and down the stairs. It took a second for those on the attack to regain composure at the audacity of the fourth hooded man. A couple started pursuing the escapee, but by the time they reached the ground floor, they couldn't see him anywhere. It seemed he had simply vanished, as if the night had taken and gulped its own.

The identified three could do nothing but wait for the call to the campus police, the dean of students and the president. All three were columnists of *The University Review*.

The story made the front page of The University newspaper. Despite the uproar, the three students would not name the fourth who'd escaped. Their discipline would be less severe, The University promised, if they cooperated. They wouldn't. They were expelled. *The University Review* rapped the decision, questioning why the international students who burned a cross on the president's lawn hadn't been expelled and calling the decision "rash and intended to pacify angry students standing on the fringe of history."

Besides the three expelled students, only two others knew the identity of the fourth hooded man. Dwayne knew of his identity because he had provided help to the escapee. I knew because Dwayne told me. From him, I learned the details. After John Owens broke free from his assailants and descended the stairs, he ran down the hallway, looking for an exit. But he realised he couldn't do that without being caught, as the pursuers would soon come down the stairs. He had to find close refuge. He stopped, looked to his left and saw, stuck on a door, a message board bearing Dwayne's name. My friend Dwayne. In the adrenaline-filled moment, John concluded that my friendship with Dwayne was his only hope, even if a thin one. John couldn't think of any other choice. He tried the knob on

Dwayne's door. It wasn't locked. John removed his hood, opened the door and stepped into Dwayne's room. Dwayne, suffering from a cold, was lying in bed, reading. He looked up at John, white gowned with the hood in one hand. Dwayne tensed, perceiving a threat and imagining his course of defense (or offense, if needed). But the fear marring John's face was clear. John closed the door, descended to his knees and whispered, "They will kill me. Please help me. Please." It was an urgent request, full of anxiety.

Dwayne rose from the bed, still suspicious. Then he heard the voices and hurried feet in the hallway and began to believe that John was in some sort of trouble. Rather than screen his actions through his mind, he acted on a protective instinct. Without speaking, Dwayne locked his door and turned off the lights. Neither man spoke for a long time. After a while, they heard voices in the hallway.

"Where could he be?"

"Don't know, man."

"Think he could be hiding somewhere?"

"You want to check the rooms?"

They went from room to room. "Is he in?" They heard a voice outside Dwayne's door.

"He's sick, man. Leave him alone."

They moved on. Dwayne waited another four hours. Except for John's whispered confession to Dwayne, neither man spoke in those hours, which were chilled by John's fear and Dwayne's confusion. Dwayne walked down the hallway and came back to tell John, "You've got to leave through the window. It's all quiet now, but you've got to be careful."

"Thanks, man," John whispered. "You don't know how much I appreciate this."

"Yeah, better hurry and get out of here before it gets too late."

Dwayne opened the window. John put his head out to ensure there was no one in sight. Then he leaped out of the window. Without his hood and gown he looked like any student out late partying.

Dwayne would tell me because I'd been the only link between John and himself. "See what your friend did? I should've turned him over so his ass would get kicked out of here."

"Why didn't you?"

"I don't know, Jojo. I guess for some reason I kind of felt sorry for him."

John would call later. "I need to tell you, Jojo, because I met Dwayne through you. I did something terrible and he helped me. Thank you!"

"What did you do?"

"I can't say."

But he must have known that I knew. He must have expected Dwayne to tell me. Perhaps by thanking me he hoped to assure my silence? Besides that I could think of nothing but one word: Trust. Either he trusted that I wouldn't divulge the information or he wanted to test me. If so, it was a mighty gamble, I thought. On what basis would he put such trust in me or expose me to such a risky test? Or perhaps he wanted to be expelled? Was he guilty that he'd escaped when his compatriots hadn't? If he trusted me, I passed. If he gambled, he succeeded. If he wanted me to tell, he failed. I shuddered to think of what he'd done, but it seemed to me that he'd be better served if I kept his confidence.

Going forward, a bond of secrecy was built between us. I would think of it this way: Dwayne had rescued him and kept the secret; I gained the knowledge and kept the secret; and John received the benefit of those acts. But even Dwayne and I healed in a way by having our finger on the trigger that could expel John from The University and not pulling it, the redemptive healing derived from aiding those that may be at odds with us such that the conscience is no longer heavily burdened by the voice urging revenge. There was a spark of hope in this, even if a tiny one, in that with this act we had opened up an opportunity for unburdened friendship. It was an opportunity for a beginning. I phoned home. It seemed an opportune time. This was after all time for making connections and reconnections.

Ten

I called home looking for sustenance, the break up with Norah still paining me. As usual I was in a hurry for fear of running up the bill: the financial chains of a poor student. Mama delayed my early exit, however. There was something – call it an intuitive connection between mother and son – that warned me she was upset. She didn't have to say it. "Mama, is there a problem?" ... That deep pause, burdened with breath...

"Your Uncle Kusi was arrested yesterday." Mama paused again... "He's feared dead."

The world went into a big, fast-spinning motion. Unbelievable. "Mama, what are you saying? Uncle Kusi is dead?"

"That's what we believe, Jojo."

"How?" Now it was I whose breath was rushing, as if that would rescue meaning from the meaningless.

"There was an attempted coup this morning." Mama's voice sounded like a distant echo. "... The fighting was heavy, but brief. When we woke up this morning, it was all over the news. They say he was part of the conspirators... they say he wanted to overthrow the government... "

The sentences sounded incoherent to me, like little pieces of a bizarre jigsaw puzzle. "Conspirators? Why would he want to overthrow the government? He's a businessman, not a politician or soldier. It doesn't make sense to me."

"The government says he financed the coup; that he hoped to be named president."

"So they killed him?"

"We don't know if it was intentional or not, but that's what we believe. There are some reports that he resisted arrest and was shot. The government hasn't confirmed or denied it."

It was still senseless to me. I knew Uncle Kusi was interested in politics, but a coup? More than a history lesson, Uncle Kusi would tell me about Ghana. "You know how we got our name? Ghana is named after a medieval West African empire renowned for its gold. The kings, reputedly full of splendour, were usually adorned with gold. It is believed that some of our people in modern Ghana migrated here from the Western Sahara region where old Ghana used to be. You see, it appears ours is a history of migration, good and bad, conquests and defeats. In all, it's a history to be proud of. In the fifteenth century, the Portuguese arrived on the shores of present day Ghana and found so much gold. They gave Elmina its name, you know. They called it Mina, which means mine. The English would later call the territory they acquired the Gold Coast. The Portuguese built the Elmina Castle around 1482 as a fort for trade, including trade in slaves. Others would follow: the Dutch, English, Danes and Swedes. Eventually, though, they left; until the English were the only ones remaining, declaring the Gold Coast a crown colony in 1874.

"From the beginning, the English faced stiff opposition from the Asantes, who fought and defeated the British in numerous wars. It wasn't until 1900 during the Yaa

Asantewaa war that the English, after much fortification, managed to defeat the Asantes with the help of some locals. Following that, in 1901, they added Asante and the Northern territories to their protectorate."

Uncle Kusi seemed to glimmer when he told of the movement towards independence.

"The movement actually took off after the Second World War. Ghanaians, or if you prefer, locals from the Gold Coast had fought at the behest of the British. Here they were, having fought against oppression and yet denied basic rights in their own land of birth. The veterans of the war faced economic difficulties at home. Political leaders like Danquah and Nkrumah were organizing, Afro-Americans like Garvey and DuBois were energizing a Pan-African conscience and India and Pakistan's independence showed that African independence too was attainable. The locals agitated. I made my financial contributions to the political parties, first Danquah's United Gold Coast Convention and later Nkrumah's Convention People's Party. I was so proud when in 1948 Nii Kwabena Botwe organised a boycott of foreign goods. I felt energised when ex-servicemen marched to the Christianburg Castle in Osu to petition the English governor about their sorry lot. Three of them were shot dead. Jojo, remember and honor the names Adjetey, Attipoe and Lamptey, remember they who wanted justice and paid for it with their blood. These events would catalyze the movement until the British had to cede power and eventually grant Ghana its independence on 6th March, 1957."

He spoke so proudly of the leaders who led the struggle at great risk to themselves. "How can I not make monetary contributions to their parties?" he asked. He spoke on occasion about actually entering politics "to clean up the mess some of our politicians are making of our great country." And he'd occasionally say that he and I could rule the country someday. For the most part, though, he concentrated on his businesses. He'd worked so hard for his success and his connections included access to the highest echelons of power. I'd have thought he wanted it that way. Why be involved in a coup? At it turned out, Mama's fears were confirmed when the government later indicated that he'd been killed in a scuffle with his captors. That was the official version of the matter and none could prove otherwise. Unofficially, however, he learned there'd been a coup attempt, but he'd played no part in it. The government, thinking him too powerful (money, influence, charisma and popularity), had already marked him as a potential threat. On the morning of the coup attempt, they decided to move against him. The goal had been to arrest him, but in the senseless execution of the orders, a group of drunken soldiers had miscarried their orders and shot him. In the aftermath of his death, his assets and bank accounts were confiscated to the state for his *sedition*.

Uncle Kusi, once looming so large, became a tiny footnote in the cacophonous history of the country. This was a single death, but it was momentous to me. It meant all to me. It was like the loss of a father many times over. I wept continually for a long time. I would not be consoled. I blamed myself for leaving Uncle Kusi to die. I got drunk, but found no prolonged solace in that. For days, I almost didn't speak. Ed tried to console me. His efforts failed. I blamed Ghana for killing Uncle Kusi. Once I blamed Ghana, I lost confidence in the country. A knee-jerk reaction? In hindsight, perhaps, yes. But it didn't feel so at that time. To me, it was not just the death of a man, but a symbol of great potential violently and forever stifled by force; not just the brutality and injustice of what happened to Uncle Kusi, but also the docile acceptance of the people. How could my Uncle Kusi be rendered so inconsequential? Was this the country to which I wanted to return after graduation? Check. A man had died. A dream had died. It seemed time for new beginnings. America had openings. Not yet checkmate.

I resigned as president of the International Students Association as the school year came to a close. My presidency had been unremarkable, full of cultural events and no more. Mburu graduated that spring. "I'm going back home," he said. "Home is where I belong. I will never belong here." Succinctly, he summed up a conclusion, whose justification lay in his four-year stay in America. A lot of thinking and deep analysis had framed that conclusion.

Freshly wounded by Uncle Kusi's death, I rejected it. "America has a lot of opportunities," I concluded.

"For some of them. For some of you."

And a week after he graduated, Mburu was gone, living only in my memory and the contact information inscribed in my address book. Yannis graduated as well, leaving campus to return to Greece. He had become a recluse after the Brewer-Castro incident, hardly seen around campus and never attending ISA meetings. I never heard from him again. I had wanted to congratulate him before he left campus, but he rebuffed me. He and I were still boxing old ghosts. Ed went home to work at the local pool house for the summer, "To meet chicks and get laid," he explained. He invited me to go home with him. I declined, not wishing to strain his family (and familiarity) for such a long period. Dwayne went home to find something to do over the time. Tanya and Dwayne treated me to dinner the night before they left campus. "If you get bored, come visit me," Dwayne said. John went to work for a senator in DC, having temporarily suspended his journalism.

I spent the summer on The University campus, which, rid of almost all students, became a hollow shadow of itself. I worked full time at the campus cafeteria, which remained open to serve the several summer workshops held on campus. Mornings and afternoons, I worked in the dish room or behind a counter serving breakfast and lunch. I spent the evenings walking aimlessly, day-dreaming (or night-dreaming?), visiting The University Pond, writing letters to parents and friends, wishing I hadn't been so rash with Marjorie, reading a book or two and generally getting bored. I longed for the fall and school, despite its headaches. I needed something to fill my time. There was nothing I found meaningful except memories of Uncle Kusi, Marjorie and Norah. I tried to contact a distant relative in Chicago to no avail. It was a long summer of long thoughts and deep memories, loneliness and tempered expectations.

Eleven

I was overjoyed when school started that fall. Classes, cramming and intramural soccer competed and almost replaced my long thoughts. Dwayne returned to campus obsessed with joining the Alpha Fraternity, asking that I do likewise. He had met some alumni who belonged to the fraternity who convinced him he ought to join. He came calling, asking me to pledge. A fraternity? "This is all black folk," he explained. "None of the foolishness of the white frats." I said I wasn't interested, but he insisted. "The brothers will love you for it," he said. Ought I to try to assimilate a bit more? This was the haunting question. I had little knowledge of the Alpha Fraternity. I'd been to a few of its parties and not found myself engaged. But it was one thing to operate on the fringes, on its alien wings and another to be in the middle of the action, a full part of the brotherhood. The latter, especially under Dwayne's entreaty, seemed more enticing at that moment. This would give me a sense of belonging, a group dedicated to me and vice versa. It could be a family away from home. At his behest – Dwayne seemed to have influence everywhere – I was invited to pledge the Alpha Fraternity. I was one of a select group of ten. This was an honour denied many others.

Still, "I'm not sure I want to do this," I kept telling Dwayne. He asked me over to his room. He poured me a half glass full of bourbon and one for himself. At first, he seemed to just want to while away the time, but then, like a prelude to a film, the generalities segued to the specific and he ventured into a bit of his past. I learned so much about the man in those thirty minutes or so that he spoke.

Dwayne Dray was conceived in 1946 in New York City, his father, a man who prided himself on being a part of the Harlem Renaissance. The man had written a few poems that were published in WEB DuBois' *The Crisis*. He was on a first name basis with Langston Hughes, whose poems he loved most among the many other poets he befriended. He listened to the speeches of James Weldon Johnson and read the books of Zora Neale Hurston. He relaxed at The Cotton Club, where performances by Cab Calloway and Duke Ellington moved him. He heard recitals by Paul Robeson at The Greenwich Village Theatre. "These form my muse," he would say. His star was brightening. He was proud to be part of what he considered would be the reinvention of the American Negro. As a poet, he saw no better way to showcase Black America's talents than through the arts. Make that Arts. James Dray was an artist who, through the creative process, was making his contribution to his people. So he thought. So he believed. His poetry was hailed by his compatriots as original, daring and ingenious. But he had a secret. James Dray was an alcoholic. In fact, he did his best work under the influence of hard liquors. He had a hard time at it when sober. One night, drunk and incoherent, he seduced and bedded the seventeen year old waiter he'd been eyeing at one of the diners he frequented in Harlem. It wasn't lovemaking –

that implied something gentler and more romantic. It wasn't lustful sex – that implied something cruder. It was a quick lay meant to sate a longing spurred on by the alcohol he'd imbibed and the looks of the seventeen-year-old Sallie Mae. It was her first time. For him, it was meant to be the only time with her. But she got pregnant.

James Dray would take care of the baby, he decided. It was his duty. But he was too young, too ambitious, to marry and be handicapped by its demands. (James Dray was thirty-two at the time.) He tried numerous jobs to raise funds to care for the baby yet to be born, but he was too deep an alcoholic to maintain any. He was fired from the library, the bookstore and the restaurant – the menial jobs he was offered. Three months after Sallie Mae got pregnant, James Dray jumped from a building to his death. Sallie Mae didn't believe it was suicide. Someone pushed him, she insisted: They envied his talent.

Pregnant with nowhere to turn, she boarded a bus and headed to Detroit to live with her aunt, who'd raised her after her mother died when Sallie Mae was ten. Dwayne Dray was born into a family of uncles, aunts and cousins in a jammed house of twelve. Times were hard. Summers were long and uneventful; winters were longer and cold. Both were filled with hunger. Spring and fall were variations of the same. In such a large family, he being the second youngest, Dwayne had to struggle for just about everything. His mother wanted better for him, though. She would read him his father's poems. He had no choice. She made him listen, even memorise them. They were full of Black pride, inspiring and uplifting. But Dwayne was drifting into the streets. Sallie Mae was gone most of the time cleaning homes, trying to save money to raise her son.

Could the cogent poetic powers of a dead father replace the tactile parental hand? The void was palpable. Dwayne found the streets and loved them. He was only twelve when his cousin Jesse introduced him to pot and sex. They would stay out in the busy streets of Detroit, pick pockets or shoplift and sell the stolen items, go get a hit and bed a prostitute or two. The streets were claiming him. His cousin was only five years older, but both boys, battered by drugs and the demands of their life-style, looked older than they were. Jesse joined a gang soon afterwards, looking for more action, more adventure. His goal was to get Dwayne into the gang in a couple of years. Dwayne looked forward to the day. But two things happened. Jesse was shot, shooter unidentified. Dwayne was shaken. Death had been a remote afterthought at best. And especially he'd never imagined it would happen to Jesse, his mentor, his idol. Still, Dwayne was developing sangfroid from walking the streets and Jesse's death alone wouldn't have stopped him. But then Sallie Mae got married to a preacher who was as strict as scripture. She moved with Dwayne into his household. The man, almost sixty, had never had children. But he was vigorous and oversaw Dwayne as he would his flock. There was resistance, but Dwayne could not match the stamina of the older Pastor Jamison whose parental code comprised a strict curfew, supervised lessons, restored poetry reading and most importantly, fatherly love shown in the manner he spoke of Dwayne to his friends.

In months, Dwayne's grades were back up, he was attending church regularly, calling the pastor Pa and in bed no later than ten. He played in the high school football team and joined the Drama Club. He was even elected class president. "You know, Jojo, when Ma married Pa Jamison," Dwayne said, "I hated the thought. I would have killed him if I had the guts, but today I'm so thankful for the love he had for me."

We drank the bourbon in near silence the rest of that evening. When I left Dwayne's room, I had decided. I belonged with him in the Alpha Fraternity.

At the first meeting, the president of the fraternity, Sean Johnson, standing under a massive poster of Malcolm X, outlined the process in general terms. For the first three weeks of our pledge period, we were to talk to no one but our fellow *pledgees* and members of the Alpha Fraternity. We couldn't even talk to friends. "No one!" Brother Sean ordered. There would be severe consequences if we disobeyed. We would all have our heads shaved clean, wear the same black tee shirt to be provided us by the fraternity, have our meals at the cafeteria as a group and generally spend most of the next month together. It was to be a month of solidarity. We had to learn the value of trusting one another. The rest of what would happen after we passed the initial test would be revealed to us in due course. We were immediately marched to the basement of the fraternity house and our heads shaved. Then we received our tee shirts. The pledging had started.

Immediately, I believed I'd made a mistake. How was I to survive a whole month so incommunicado? I understood and even applauded the reason behind it, the discipline, the solidarity. It seemed also to signal to all *outsiders* a message of self distinction and reliance, even pride. But did I have the courage and strength to send that message? The first day of the pledge was difficult. We marched together in a file just about everywhere. I did my best to ignore the stares. Ed tried to talk to me. I ignored him, pretending I couldn't hear him. (Good thing we were no longer roommates, having moved to single rooms in our second year.) Outwardly I succeeded, but I burned inwardly with discomfort. The next evening we were marched to do drills. I was forced to yell louder than I'd ever before and got hoarse. Even in that brief period, I was drawn to my fellow pledgees, knowing the circumstances and difficulties of our fate, the empathy of sharing it ... In that period, I could see the larger world drawing away, almost like an enemy field, but I had to tolerate the drift lest my mission to become a part of the Alpha Fraternity be compromised.

Still, I struggled with the process and made a decision that night. The next day we gathered in front of the fraternity house to march together to breakfast. I was sixth in line. Before Brother Sean gave his orders, I moved to the front, ignoring the rage appearing on his face. It seemed intended to intimidate and intimidated I was, but I had to do it.

"Brother Jojo, under what authority do you leave your place?"

"Big Brother Sean ..."

"Shut up! Who gave you permission to speak?"

"No one, Big Brother Sean."

"I can't hear you."

"No one, Big Brother Sean!!!"

He stared at me, fuming. I had to believe part of it was just acting. There couldn't be that much rage in there. "Speak!" he ordered.

"Big Brother Sean, I have decided to withdraw from the pledge!!!"

My compatriots gasped. I wasn't sure if Big Brother Sean was angry or disappointed or surprised. Perhaps it was a combination of all three. His voice was no longer loud. Now, it was transformed into a low, even soft voice, indicating to me something furious held in check. "What?" He'd heard me, but this wasn't a part of the script. "You're going to quit?"

I didn't like that word *quit*, but felt disinclined to argue semantics. "Yes!"

He didn't ask me why or attempt to reason with me. Rather, he stared at me for what must have been at least a full minute. In the seconds comprising that time, I thought I saw anger transform to disappointment and disappointment give to pain (or something akin to that). "Leave!"

I did, but heard him say to the rest, "This is a test of manhood. There's no room for you if you don't have what it takes to prove you're a man."

I'd realised that no matter how enticing the prospect of belonging to the Alpha Fraternity, I couldn't so completely alienate myself from the rest of the campus, nor could I cede such complete control over my autonomy, even if for a mere month. I felt free, so free when I left the pledgees, though knowing the contempt that might be heaped on me. But it went beyond that. Dwayne refused to talk to me, even after the pledge was over and he could talk to whomsoever he chose. He only said, "You know what trouble I had to go through to get you invited?" Then he was gone. He didn't respond to my salutations or the notes I sent him apologizing for my conduct.

While I dealt with this crisis in my friendship with Dwayne, Ed reached a new level of happiness in his college career. It seemed his goal to bed as many women as he could, which had begun in the latter part of the first year, now materialised fully. I would see him with a different woman each time we met. He'd tell me over lunch how he took them to his single room and "screwed them." "Jojo, they all want it as much as we do," he said. I could make no similar report to him. The entire world seemed closed. My relationship with the bulk of the black community had chilled after I walked away from the Alpha Fraternity. The tension was never easy, but it now was worse. News of my withdrawal having spread, Joan blasted me when we met and even Tanya registered her disapproval. "You shouldn't have started and quit, Jojo," she said.

Could I complain? Had I not made the rejection and therefore, invited the backlash? And to whom could I go for comfort? I couldn't turn to Ed. How could he understand? He had his comfort and rested blithely in its zones. John was completely out of the question. So while Ed partied and paraded his sexual exploits, I watched him with envy. He tried to set me up, in fairness to him. But inevitably my attempts ended without success. Either the women were completely uninterested (which alienated me) or interested in a curious way, more like an exploration of a myth than a person (which insulted me). Either way, we never made it anywhere, Ed's ladies and I. After a series of rejections, I no longer accepted his invitations to honour dates he tried to set up for me. How could one man shoulder the burden of so many rejections? My confidence crushed under its impact. And in the meantime Mama and Papa were writing and telling me to come home and pick a wife. "I'm still in school," I complained. "Never too soon," they insisted.

As for John, he roamed the campus apparently looking for a mission. Having suspended his writing for *The*

University Review, it seemed he was derailed. He joined clubs: debate, ski, rowing, tennis...I could fill a page with the clubs that occupied his time. On occasion, he'd invite me to his apartment to share some beer and play Beatles' songs. His unicorn still hung on his living room wall and he continued to adjust it, looking for it to hang perfectly.

But all these sometimes seemed so far removed. It appeared I was a ghost living in a land of flesh and blood, confined to the fringes, sometimes loved, sometimes disliked; now welcome, now feared. In my own skin, which I found so comfortable, I was perplexed by it all. I needed to escape for a while, which is why I felt so relieved when I got into the Language Study Abroad programme in Arles, France the next summer.

France allowed me to leave a lot behind and concentrate on learning another language. It was a short programme of ten intense weeks. I was placed with a family in Arles in the Provence region. I was only allowed to speak French with them, which was extremely difficult at first. There was a lot of gesturing and signaling at the dinner table. Unknown and without the dictates of a regulated schedule besides attending classes, I roamed Arles. I saw the hotel where Van Gogh had stayed. I stood by the Loire, was awed by the grandiosity of the local amphitheatre and took a train trip to neighbouring Avignon. The days passed quickly. Most days I was either in class with the rest of the group from The University studying French literature, grammar and civilization, or roaming the streets with my classmates or studying and doing my homework. I went with a couple of my mates to Marseille, Nice, Cote d'Azur, Bordeaux and Carcassone.

I visited Chamonix and took the cable car to Mont Blanc, awed by the expanse of the snow-blanketed mountains of the Alps. And then on to Geneva for a day, where the fountain on the Rhone transfixed me. For a brief while I seemed to have moved beyond the haunts of the past. There was a serenity to be derived in the changed scenery, like a blank page without the chore of a script written with experience.

We had a brief midterm holiday, during which I went to Barcelona. I was among a group of six – all Americans, except me. We filed past the official at the Spanish border. All went by without incident, except me. At the sight of the American passports, my colleagues were allowed to pass without further inspection. I was detained a few minutes and my Ghanaian passport scrutinised. Alienated among aliens. *No escape, Jojo.* "What was that all about?" my friends asked. I could have asked that question myself. (*Ladies and Gentlemen, how much time do you have, for my story is long indeed? I was taught summary in school, but if you want the full story, I will have to forgo all skills of summary.*) We spent three days in Barcelona, mostly looking around, drinking and eating.

My French improved and it got much easier to communicate with my host family. Then the programme was over and we had to return to America. I took a train to Nice for my flight to the US through London. At London's Heathrow Airport, my luggage was subjected to a criminal's scrutiny. Even my shoes were taken to be tested. (And this was way before we had the threat of so called shoe-bombers.) I observed that none of my American colleagues were questioned.

When I returned for my third year, things changed a little. Time may have healed matters a bit: Dwayne invited me to lunch, the excuse being to celebrate the award of the Nobel Prize to Martin Luther King, Jr. as well as President Lyndon Johnson's signing of the Civil Rights Act of 1964. After expressing his hope in the Act and pride over the award, he told me of his hurt when I rejected the Alpha Fraternity. "It wasn't just personal. It was a rejection of the black community."

I apologized again. I only did what I believed was right for me at the time, with no other agendum. He knew, Dwayne said. He'd thought it over and realised it wasn't worth losing a friendship. "By the way," he said, "Tanya and I just broke up." Unbelievable. I asked why. "I don't know, brother. We just fell apart." (Perhaps it was due to his womanising? Dwayne never made much mention of it, but everyone knew it.) He tried to act bravely, as if it didn't matter to him, but his disguise was too shallow. I hoped he wasn't renewing our friendship solely to fill a void left by Tanya. But it wouldn't matter anyway. I had missed him. I made it a point to call him from time to time, to have lunch or go for a beer. I told him I needed a woman. He said he'd set me up. "With the right person," he said. "I promise you. No Joan or Deirdre."

It wasn't until much later that he fulfilled that promise.

Meantime, I continued on the same autopilot: ordering pizza on Saturday nights with some friends from the International Students Association, watching television movies; staying up late and sometimes missing classes in the morning because I was too tired; playing soccer from time to time with some of the ISA members while our American friends teased us that the real sport was

American football; going to work and then classes and then more classes and work; spending many midterm breaks or vacations on campus and getting bored; eyeing and lusting after long-legged women and finding them unresponsive; watching Ed, Phoebe and their friends protest the Vietnam War and the draft...

Dwayne had me over to his room when Malcolm X was assassinated. There were about six of us there. He turned off the lights and lit a number of candles. "He was a great, misunderstood American," Dwayne said. "He embodied all that Black America had to say to White America, but was afraid to say. He told White America what it needed to know, but was afraid to know." Phoebe and Ed both condemned the killing. "I didn't agree with him at first," Phoebe said, "But he seemed to be changing, recognizing that white people are not devils, that blacks and whites can live together."

"Is that why they killed him, you think?" Ed asked.

"I don't know," said Phoebe. "What I know is that this killing won't solve anything for anybody."

"What's this country coming to?" Ed wondered among other things, Martin Luther King, Jr's civil rights march from Selma to Montgomery; race riots in Los Angeles that resulted in thirty-five deaths; and protests at the Vietnam War held outside the White House. Our lives centred on campus and observation of the events around us with some of us protesting from time to time. We all seemed to be looking for something.

And then Ed met Jenny Arnold. Like a full stop, she ended his wild ways. I'd heard of women changing men, but never believed it until then. Ed complained, "She won't give me no action. But I love her, man." I couldn't believe Ed could fall in love and stay celibate. I was wrong. They'd met in a philosophy class. If ever love at first sight could be proved, theirs would be the prototype. They became inseparable from the first day of class when they sat next to each other. Soon, Ed cut his hair short and shaved his beard and moustache. It was hard for me to determine what attracted them to each other. She was from a rich, conservative family in Boston, her politics matched her upbringing and she was staunchly Christian and believed that America could do no wrong. The only thing they seemed to have in common was wealth, but where Ed saw it as an embarrassment, she embraced it and asserted it as her right. While there was no arguing these things with her, she never sought to impose her views. So long as you didn't challenge her way of life or manner of thinking, she was willing to live and let live. This way, I presume she managed to date Ed while accommodating his views. By extension, Ed's friends who were willing to abide by her code of mutual stalemate (myself among them) were within her good graces. But the more radical were pushed to the fringes. Phoebe and others, for instance, began to shrink from Ed's circle of friends.

I admired their relationship, this union of seeming opposites so well harmonised. I envied him and wanted what they shared. But where would I find mine? I hadn't fully wrestled Norah away, but I managed to hold her image at bay most of the time. She seemed to have developed her own tactics: to forgive by ignoring. She hardly looked at me when we crossed paths. When I greeted her, she responded lukewarmly and moved away. I even called her once in the third year, when after a party and unsuccessful attempts to get laid, I remembered the time we'd spent and believed, in my tipsy mind, that we could still offer something to each other. But she had turned cold. She was well. She didn't ask about me. I did the questioning and she answered monosyllabically. I felt cheated by the conversation. Once I walked into the cafeteria where she was eating by herself. I thought this an opportunity. She didn't oppose it when I suggested sitting with her, but it was with indifference as neutral as it was uninviting. I'd hardly warmed up thoughts for conversation, when two women walked in and went and sat in a corner nearby. "If you don't mind," said Norah, "I'll go sit with Eve and Sue." I walked out of the cafeteria feeling foolish, seeking answers, groping, tempted yet taunted by colour, I came to the conclusion that she'd react differently if my skin were the same colour as hers (and that I too would have acted differently). Or was she, with her passive-aggression, proclaiming somewhat self-righteously her rightness and my wrongness in taking the initiative to break up our relationship and giving me no ease of conscience for that action? "But Norah," I wanted to yell, "if you blame me, blame me for weakness, not ill intent. Ought you not lay the gravest blame on the heads of those who exposed my weakness?" I was injured like a wounded warrior waiting in ambush, waiting for the opportune time to exact revenge, like a famished scavenger circling patiently, unnoticed, calm. Dangerous. Norah never offered me the opportunity.

"I envy you," I confessed to Ed.

"Your time will come," he said.

I wondered, though, if mine would indeed ever come.

Twelve

It did. The day I met Fiona Harris... Or shall I say night? It was at a small party organised by Dwayne sometime in the last fall of my college years. I entered Dwayne's room to the sound of Ray Charles's *Hit The Road, Jack*. I forced a nervous smile, but said nothing. "Come in brother. Here's Leroy and Marc. And there's Fiona." I shook each hand and sat down, the gulf between us narrowed and shortened. I still hated these contradictions, but how does one escape them? This love and non-love, closeness and distance, alikeness and deep difference, oneness and separation. After so many years and all we'd experienced together, Dwayne and I still faced that vexing chasm. I tried to will it away, but it wouldn't be willed away. And for long minutes I felt lost, not knowing how to fit into the conversation. It was as if they were speaking an entirely different language completely beyond my comprehension. Yet it was English, English that had evolved into a vernacular of its own. And they were speaking of experiences I felt were outside my reach, that I couldn't relate to: being stopped on the streets by cops for being black, predatory lending practices targeted at them, neighbourhoods they would not be allowed to live in, a different depiction in the media, the slant of a society's bias against their success; generally the formidable challenge of succeeding in the

US in black skin ... I was getting bored. Was this the party that Dwayne promised? Was this a party of five to talk about matters of remote relevance to me? Four were active in the room, but because I was not a full participant, I felt almost invisible, like an unneeded apendage. I was quiet, searching for the moment when I'd say my goodbye and leave. I decided to wait another thirty minutes to end this road of social interaction that seemed to meander endlessly.

But within those thirty minutes I noticed something about Fiona – a vague familiarity in her manner of speaking, her accent – a sense of a memory that didn't quite seem authentic but still required attention. I stole fleeting glances at her, hoping not to be too obvious. I enjoyed her looks, which begged to be studied – her thin eyes, slender nose and full lips, her slim but robust frame. After many failed attempts, I forced down my anxiety and asked her, "What year are you ... Fiona?"

"Oh, I'm sorry," said Dwayne. "Fiona's not a student."

"I'm an administrative assistant at the Admissions Office," she said.

"And guess what?" interjected Dwayne. "She's from Ghana. Just like you, Jojo." I had looked hard at her when I noticed that sense of familiarity in her speech and now Dwayne's comment forced me to look harder. But why had Dwayne tormented me with the delay of such vital information? Something began to brew and it smelled fresh.

I knew the course of the race I was running had to change. I couldn't let this chance slip. I was impressed by Fiona's knowledge of Ghana. Hindsight informs me that I was hungry for that impression, yearning for connection and familiarity. And I found Fiona an attractive introduction to the otherwise alienating landscape called America. I was still like a strange creature fallen from outer space, establishing at the onset an otherness that abided. But Fiona promised me an opening and tactile refreshment. Now I knew what it must feel for a man travelling a wasteland to find an oasis and not a mere mirage teasing and disappearing like some magician's crude trick. Not Joan. Not Phoebe. Not Norah. Not even Marjorie. Fiona! When that apparent embodiment of Ghana was introduced to me, that Ghanaian-ness unexpectedly revealed (but this time like a pleasing, divine work), I couldn't let her go. Sure, this wasn't a big opening but it held the promise of one. After all, as she revealed to me, she'd been mostly raised in Washington DC. She was American and intended to remain so. Her quickness to disavow Ghana should have been a warning to me. But, like a wide-eyed fish, I was already hooked by the sumptuous bait. There was no escape. The Ghanaian bit seemed like a showpiece to be dusted off from time to time when needed and then hoarded back in the closet for a future date. Despite all that, though, she had a softness for things Ghanaian, albeit a malleable softness. That she'd marry a Ghanaian, however, was the farthest thing from her mind. After she'd left Ghana with her father, Ghanaian stepmother and half sister, she'd never returned. I offered her something in common with her new maternal roots: something akin to her stepmother (the living mother she'd become so close to, whose connections she now could not severe simply because of the lack of blood ties between them). But as I'd learn later that was as far as she'd go. Resettling in Ghana was out of the equation.

In my view, my courtship began the night I met her in Dwayne's room. I was too bashful to ask for her number then, but she stayed in my mind because of the heartfelt impression she left on me, like a stubborn idea rethought again and again. If that were all, though, I might have moved beyond her. She had spread from that mental confine into every pulse and heartbeat, it seemed. Norah hadn't reached such depths, not even Marjorie. It was a powerlessness I could only maintain under the grip of a compelling coyness worsened because I didn't want to jeopardise any prospects I might have with her. When I met her again around campus, I was playing soccer at The University Park. I noticed that she stopped, stood and watched. I was drawn by that show of attention (whether in me or the game) and it was sufficient pretext to excuse myself from the game and go to her. "Do you like soccer?" was my lame question, asked with the hope to begin something.

"Kind of. They play it a lot in Ghana."

"You're right about that."

"I see you've got some pretty sharp moves." She smiled.

"Thanks."

"Your friends are waiting for you. I shouldn't keep you from your game."

"It's all right. We're just playing around."

"I see. Well, I've got to get going anyway. I've got to get back to work."

It took all the courage I had (and some I didn't know I had) to ask, "Do you mind if I call you sometime?" It was a difficult moment, as hard as a dilemma that I could overcome only by pretending the consequence of a rejection wasn't important. She hesitated a second, for me a doubled perpetuity, then gave me her number. But I didn't call. Fear! Fear that must find its excuses. I recollected the moment when she gave me the number, thinking that she'd done it hesitatingly. Didn't she seem to wear a sneer as well? Based on that, I feared the rejection that would follow if I called her for a date. I planned all week, but couldn't find an antidote to that apprehension. Yet, on the next Friday night, I bought a bottle of wine, although the cost of it on my measly income rendered me almost bankrupt for a while. My logic was that if I bought the wine, I would be forced to put it to use.

I dialed Fiona's number, but hung up when she picked up the phone and said hello. *Oh Fear, how I hate thee, thou monster and master of inaction.* Again the fear offered its excuse: it seemed she'd put too much emphasis on the *hell* in the hello. I was confused. I tried to see Mburu. I'd forgotten he'd graduated and returned to Kenya. Ed wasn't home. Desperate, I went to see John and confessed. He seemed so relieved, perhaps even grateful, that I'd come to seek his help. He gave me three shots of vodka that rendered me a bit tipsy, especially because I hadn't eaten supper. Still nervous, but slightly more courageous, my chest beating uncomfortably, I walked to Fiona's off-campus apartment. I knocked on the door with the nervousness and liquor in combat. I debated the expedient option of fleeing as I waited for a response. In fact, I was on the verge of doing so, staying only because she opened the door quicker than I could get away. She looked surprised to see me. This is a horrible mistake, I thought.

"Jojo!" she exclaimed. "Come on in." I walked in. "How are you?"

"I'm fine. And yourself?" My speech was controlled by the anxiety.

"Not bad."

We both said nothing. I knew she was expecting me to announce the reason behind my intrusion, but I didn't know what to say or how to say it, whatever that *it* might be.

"Can I get you some water or something?"

"Oh." I realised how awkward I must have looked standing in front of her with a bottle of wine in one hand and saying nothing. "I...I brought you a bottle of wine."

She took it. "Thanks." She studied the bottle. "To what do I owe this generous gesture?"

A bolder man would have announced to her the reason: my interest in her. How complicated could that be? A man of words would have said it craftily: something smooth about her looks, something about missing her or a witty expression to make her laugh and think. A man of action would have done something meaningful: something like taking her hand and kissing it. But I was none of those – not at that moment – so I said, "Nothing. I just thought you might enjoy it."

How weak, Jojo.

"Sit down," she said as she took the bottle to the kitchen. "Do you want some of this wine?"

"Please."

She opened the bottle and poured two glasses full. She sat next to me on the couch. "*A votre sante*," she toasted.

"*A la votre*," I replied. "You speak French?"

"Barely."

"I'm forgetting mine." I took a sip of wine. "I took a term in France...Foreign study programme."

"Hmm. You are such a travelled man."
"Hardly." I drank some more.
"Don't be so modest. Ghana, US, France?"
"But that's about it." I sipped even more wine.
"That's one more country than me," she said, tasting her wine.
"If you put it that way... But, you, you have such an interesting background."
"I'm getting hungry," she said. "Do you want something to eat? I was just about to fix dinner."
"Certainly."
"I can make something quick. You like spaghetti?"
"That would be nice."
She walked to the kitchen. I could soon smell the boiling spaghetti while I considered the possibilities so rife, mostly salacious, but none of which might ripen. From the living room I could see her retrieve the already prepared sauce from the fridge. I wanted so much to be close to her. I walked over and stood next to her, drawn by something that seemed to overcome all other considerations. I liked to think it was love that did the fighting, that it was love that defeated the fear. "I like to spice up the sauce a little," she said. "I guess it's part of having eaten so much spiced food in Ghana." She took out a chopping board and an onion, which she began cutting.
As I watched, she looked up and asked, "Do you cook?" Before I could respond, she was wincing and holding her index finger with blood gushing out of it. "Oh dear! I cut myself."
She held her hand, opened the faucet and was about to put her finger under the running water when I reached out for her bleeding hand. Some strange force must have been controlling my actions. I didn't know

what, but it wasn't my mind. I held Fiona's hand briefly and, as if examining it, brought it close and then put her bleeding finger in my mouth. My mind wasn't in control. I sucked the blood and she let me do so without resisting. Was this the infancy of love, that state of hearty lunacy? She watched as I sucked her blood and then, after about a minute, I released her hand and took a step forward and with her blood on my lips, kissed her, first slowly on the lips and then our mouths opened up to each other and our tongues met and they mixed our saliva and her blood. I drank deep her saliva and smelled intensely her well-scented body. She put her hands on my cheeks and her blood was over my face and for countless seconds we kissed. Then, as if she felt cheated, she bit hard on my lower lip, ignoring my moan, until my lip bled. And I didn't pull back as we continued to kiss, in our saliva and in our blood.

Unexhausted, but necessarily suspending a good thing, we pulled back. Fiona said, "Oh look, I have covered your face with blood." But her finger had stopped bleeding, except for a minor trickle.

"It's all right," I said.

She soaked a napkin in water and wiped the blood off my face. She went to the bathroom and covered her finger in a bandage. She finished the spaghetti and we ate, but that was like the anti-climatic epilogue to a suspense-filled drama.

"It's the best spaghetti I've ever had," I said, an obvious lie we both enjoyed. But not so fast... it really was the best spaghetti in that it was eaten in a state of utter exhilaration.

"You're too smooth," she said.

After dinner, we spoke until it was almost midnight. I

announced that I was leaving. "I really enjoyed the night," I said.

"Me too."

I hugged her and walked home. I thought something strange was happening to me. I liked it. I called it love. I don't know what others might call it, but I didn't care. I had never been here ever, not at this level... I'd shared of her in an unforgettable way (beginning with an accident) and she had allowed me to do so, that she had decided to share of me in like manner (on purpose), that I had watched her grimace and felt as if the knife had cut my own flesh... swallowing her blood, feeling the climb of my pulse and hers, as though her blood was running through me... and when I kissed her, it had seemed as if her blood was finally settling, finding a resting place in mine, becoming one, especially at the moment when she'd drawn blood from me into that amalgam of fluids...

The following days and weeks, we discovered each other. I wanted to know her, make her familiar like the insides of my eyelids. I watched her, smelled her, listened to her. Fiona liked to read. She read me long excerpts from novels and love poems. We took walks mostly at night when she was finished with work, my arms folded around her, our bodies against the darkness of the night. When one complained about being cold, the other held on tighter; when we went to her apartment, we would talk and make love. Forget fucking or screwing... this was making love, to put it on its deservingly sophisticated pedestal. "*Je t'aime*," I would say to her. These times, I believed, were our defining moments when abstractions of love became a reality and expectations were met. I cherished, too, the days when we would go to the park on the outskirts of campus and repose on one of its benches. I would run my fingers through her hair, tousling them a little and she would complain, affecting anger. She would place her head on my chest and I would tell her there was no woman prettier than she and she would hold on to me and we would both wish we could soar free from all and everything. We had reached into the darkened blindness without fear and reservation and discovered that beyond the blindness, there was something that had no definable contours that only the genuine and daring could find, that very few knew and fewer still understood.

Once I tried to get fresh in the park, fooled by the tranquility of our relationship. "We're alone, Fiona. We can do whatever we want."

"Yeah, but not here."

"And why not?"

"There's no privacy here. You're crazy."

I pulled her closer and moved my head in search of her lips. She didn't resist. I let my hands roam her body and when she still didn't resist I let them reach for her chest to cup her breasts. "Stop it," she said playfully but firmly.

Not that our lovemaking was that spectacularly different. To tell the truth, I think on the first go, I reached climax sooner than I should have. I'm not sure if that was due to the enduring bone-deep desire for her that made me too aroused or whether I had just become a premature ejaculator. The second time lasted longer and I brought her to climax as well. In any case, I knew a relationship (or love) has to be more than its physical expression and so nothing could replace the times we took walks in the evening, when it was as if I was alone with just her, regardless of how many people were outside.

But amid all this, a question asked itself repeatedly because it was so important to me: Was this woman from Ghana? Well, not quite. As our relationship got stronger, I learned more about her family, partly from Fiona herself. And then there were the visits I took with her to Washington DC to visit. I met her mother (or rather, step-mother), a delightful woman born and raised in Ghana whom I couldn't resist admiring. I know Ghanaians are reputed for their hospitality, but she lifted it to a higher level – into an almost perfect art form. The first time I met her, I almost felt as if I'd known her all her life. It wasn't anything she said really, just the warmth she projected, the grin spreading from lip to eye, the handshake (unlike the American version, not so firm, but still long and unhurried). She had a dignified reserve that wasn't bashful, just careful without being suspicious. She called me "My countryman" on that first visit. She was the one who showed me around the house, made sure my bed was made (as Fiona insisted that it would be improper for us to share the same bed under her parents' roof). It was she who made sure I participated at the dinner table, when the conversation swayed too much into the personal family life, by asking questions directed to me. She charmed me without knowing it.

Not that her father was far behind. He too gave me a congenial reception. He had a way about him, though, that seemed a step removed, a bit judgemental (for which I couldn't blame him as I understood that he had to gauge the worth of the man who'd been brought into their home by his beloved daughter). He was more talkative and yet he seemed to study his surroundings and those in it with suspicion. It wasn't the type of suspicion that would push others away, but the type that was designed as self-defense. Whereas her mother never ventured into it, he didn't hesitate to ask about my plans for the future. What did I want to do when I finished school? Frankly, I found that question irritating. I told him I was still thinking about it. He said nothing, but I knew he wasn't very impressed with my answer.

And then there was her sister Simone. Oh, my. Oh, my, oh, my. As they say, what a character. She seemed to have acquired an accent not quite American or Ghanaian. It had a certain flavoured quality to it, hard to place, suggesting to me that she was straining to perfect it. She didn't seem to have much interest in me. "You're from Ghana?" She shrugged dismissively when I answered yes.

Deliberately, I said, "I hope to return soon."

She rolled her eyes. "Oh, please. Why would you do that?"

She was better ignored than engaged, I decided. How she could so blatantly dismiss me, her mother and her country of conception, was beyond me. (But I had done no better than her. If she had said so boldly, I ought to reward her for honesty. I, though, was weaving and dodging, intending and retreating.)

Little by little, I was able to put together the story. Their parents had met soon after Ghana won independence from Britain in 1957. As the first country south of the Sahara to gain its independence, Ghana was seen as a beacon of hope for the rest of Black Africa, in fact for the African Diaspora. When its first leader, Kwame Nkrumah, declared that Ghana's independence would be meaningless unless linked with the total liberation of the African continent, Black America heard that call too. Black liberation. Here was the opening of an epoch of hope and pride, to be anchored by the African personality, as much a part of as it was different from the rest of humanity. Senghor and others had proclaimed Negritude, a call to reassert the history that belonged to Africa and whether credited or discredited in its depiction of blackness as a foil to whiteness, it was a loud voice. All over the continent, dashing leaders were rising to join the new march towards Pan-Africanism. The Organization of African Unity was being birthed. Kwame Nkrumah loomed large, creating the shipping line The Black Star Line (borrowing from Marcus Garvey); changing the country's name from the Gold Coast to the old Western Saharan empire name of Ghana; naming the national soccer team the Ghana Black Stars; unfurling the horizontal stripes of red, gold and green on the flag of the new Ghana and boldly inserting a black star in the middle of the gold. Nkrumah pronounced Black Americans and West Indians among Africa's greatest gifts to the world. Some of Black America took note. When Robert Lee and Sarah Lee, black doctors who'd studied with Nkrumah at the University of Pennsylvania, went to Ghana in 1957 to celebrate the country's independence then moved there with their two sons a year later, some of Black America took note. When WEB DuBois and his wife Shirley Graham were invited by Nkrumah to spend the rest of their lives in Ghana and when Dr. Hurston and his wife Dorothy went to Ghana to work with DuBois on the Encyclopedia Africana project, certain of Black America took note too.

Among them was young George Harris, a great, great grandson of slaves, graduated from Howard University with a degree in law, admirer of the Civil Rights Movement, but torn between the more aggressive portion of the movement and the non-violent resistance of others.

George Harris, then an associate professor at Howard Law School, struggled with a past that instilled caution in him, a tentative approach to the authoritative system and the desire to contribute to the movement. He couldn't reconcile the conflict, but in Ghana he saw a black nation where all he needed to do was contribute his talent, period. Here was a country of black people, run by black people. If Ghana succeeded, the rest of Black Africa would succeed; if Black Africa succeeded, the Black Diaspora had hope. The prompting for him to leave had roots in the death in Money, Mississippi of fourteen-year-old Emmett Till in August of 1955, murdered because he'd allegedly whistled at a white woman. George Harris felt sick when he saw the mutilated photos of the young man. Neither the triumph that same year of Rosa Parks' refusal to give up her bus seat to a white man or the ensuing Montgomery Bus Boycott could erase that horrific image – to be resurrected when an assembly of people protesting segregation, including schoolchildren, were met with police dogs and fire hoses capable of stripping the bark off trees. And then the murder of Medgar Evers in front of his house in June of 1963 . . . (By then, Fiona's mother had been dead seven years. Father and daughter still mourned her passing; perhaps, the challenge and thrill of Africa would numb the loss.) These killings emptied him even more. He could have embraced either the nonviolent approach of Martin Luther King or the militant stance of Malcolm X, but he felt incapable of doing so in America, which he saw as on the brink of implosion.

The young lawyer arrived in Ghana in 1963 (incidentally, the year I left for America) with his eighteen-year-old daughter. He quickly established his law practice. Here, the struggle had a different significance. It wasn't a march in the streets for the right to vote, nor was it a march to gain the right to drink from the same water fountains or defecate into the same toilets as whites. It was a two-layered struggle: first to create in the people a consciousness of the political reality against the imperial forces arrayed against them post *de jure* independence and second, to create the infrastructure and systems capable of sustaining long-term growth.

George Harris met Fiona's new mother in Ghana: Sissi, a recently widowed woman who was also mourning her loss. When she met George Harris, she was instantly struck by his idealism, his passion. Plus she identified with the way he refused to let go completely of his dead wife, just as she couldn't let go completely of her dead husband. The empathy was instantaneous, the courtship rigorous, the marriage swift (happening six months after they'd met). Fiona took full credit for the meeting between George Harris and Sissi, for, she said, had it not been for her illness they wouldn't have met – a lawyer from America and a nurse from Ghana. George Harris had previously warned Fiona about the dangers of malaria. "You've got to take your medicine," her father had entreated. But she was young and therefore, invincible. How could a tiny mosquito cause her any serious illness? Fiona didn't take her prophylactic. And only two months after she enrolled in school, malaria consumed her. She'd dismissed the chill as a passing fever, but then when she lost her appetite and felt the mighty impact of her head pain (more severe than the flu had ever given her in the United States), she knew this was serious. In no time, she was puking and barely able to leave her bed.

A panicked George Harris, hearing of his daughter's illness, picked her up from school immediately and rushed her to the Military Hospital, begging the nurses to save his only issue. Sissi calmed him. "She will be okay, Mr. Harris," she said with self-confident reassurance. This wasn't just a professional façade, however. It was too confident to be that shallow. It had to spring from that mysterious well within that calms the otherwise troubled. Both father and daughter were struck by Sissi's firm kindness and care. She would nurse two things: Fiona's illness and George Harris's love. He took her to lunch and then dinner. They would go dancing at the Lido, go shopping together at the Makola Market, sometimes at Bukom Market, share Club Beer on many nights and attend theatrical performances at the National Theatre of Ghana. On some days, they'd drive to the independence arch (Black Stare Square), where George Harris, staring at the words "Freedom and Justice" on the arch, would come close to tears and Sissi, though puzzled, was impressed by his willingness to show such vulnerability. She would come to love him in a short time, this man who was so impassioned about making a difference for the black people of the world, who believed that a progressive African country was the perfect place to start.

But George Harris would become disillusioned. The difficulty of nation-building stared straight at him. The romance with independence was gone, worn lean by the imposition of one-party rule, false and dead starts... And that wish to return home. Home is not always where the heart desires to be, after all. George Harris was finding out. For him, the seeds were implanted when he realised that he'd become like the wind, seemingly blowing forever, seemingly meant for no place. America had rejected him in so many ways. If he could halt the earth's spin, he would have seized time so he could reverse that mad spin. Let America know that he wished to be a part of it; if only that bizarre part of its history would succumb, without the continuing specter it cast on the present; if only the present could reform itself under its own founding principle of all being born equal and allow for the pursuit of that principle without any overt or covert subversion. If only he would ask America to hear his case. But he couldn't and so he'd found this new hope, a miracle from the far wilderness, a black nation under black leadership and a leader who summoned him back to lands suppressed by history and caricatured by media, but which held on to him the way even a mother calls to her lost progeny. The spiritual bridge towered over the physical rivers of space, time and distorted histories. Back home! Suddenly he needn't summon time to a standstill. He could work within it. Suddenly he wouldn't feel like an oddball amid an ocean of whiteness; suddenly he could feel at home.

But he'd not gone to Ghana under a naïve expectation that without any hesitation the country would welcome him wholeheartedly. His was a simpler expectation to belong. Period. And yet, even there, he knew his accent alone pushed him into a different zone, a zone of the foreign, that word he would rather have escaped – alien. Ghana allowed him in, but he remained at an unshakable level . . . American.

And then the society that developed within the society . . . the circle of Black American expatriates who met frequently. He'd hated it at first, but he soon realised that he needed it. It was like a temporary sanctuary where it seemed everyone understood him, at some level at least, despite whatever differences they might have had, despite the fact that he wouldn't have liked to share any space with some of them in America. But here there were so few of them that they couldn't afford to be selective. The circle of regulars comprised doctors, lawyers, artists, teachers and social workers... Each had come to Ghana for similar and different reasons, each expecting a home, each disappointed in his or her own way, each reckoning one way or the other with the reality that wasn't necessarily the dream.

That was a part of the disappointing seed. But one incident in particular completely disemboweled him: an attempt on Nkrumah's life and its aftermath. A general distrusting mood immediately descended on the country. Foreigners, in particular, became suspect. George Harris could not avoid the label. He was foreign, whether he so classified himself or not. But most disheartening was when a renowned Ghanaian pundit announced in a radio interview that black Americans were the most suspicious group of foreigners: "American Negroes in Ghana have to be watched very carefully. Think about it. They are the group most capable of infiltrating our ranks because they are black as we are. But we must remember that they are American. As Americans, who knows what they might be willing to do for American interests, for American spy agencies? And it's no secret that America dislikes Nkrumah's policies, his non-alignment, his socialist economics." There were little deaths happening to George Harris when he heard that interview. Sure, it was just one man's opinion, but how many Ghanaians felt that way? And not just that. George Harris would soon be stopped on the streets of Accra and searched like a criminal one night. Images of being stopped in American streets replayed before him. He could have cried. And in a way he did. The implosion weakened him.

All he needed was the proper prodding. It had started when Malcolm X arrived in Ghana. At a meeting with a group of black American expatriates, he got into a long conversation with George Harris. "Brother," Malcolm X said, "We need your talents back home. I appreciate what you're doing in the motherland, but we sure could use people like you in our struggle in America." At that time, George Harris felt heavily prompted to consider whether he ought to return to America. He decided to wait and see. When Nkrumah was overthrown in February 1966, the young man had had enough. He wasn't sure where the country was headed. Much as he had his differences with the Nkrumah government, he wasn't sure the new leadership was what the country needed. In fact, he feared the country was on the verge of significant bloodshed. Married to a newly pregnant Ghanaian woman, he moved back to the US with his family. With a child on the way, he had to find a steady source of income. He returned to teaching at Howard University Law School. Wasn't that the most effective way of reaching and influencing the future? Fiona's sister, Simone, was born seven months after they returned.

But what of Fiona? What did she see of the times spent in Ghana, the latter days of her teenage years, when she had gone there, first to finish secondary school and then as a student at the University of Ghana? At first the sight of so many of her kind thrilled her. Unlike the United States where white was dominant, here black was it. The white power had just been dislodged. But, her perceptions changed when she realised that the change she expected was happening too slowly, when it seemed the people ascribed more value to things foreign, where some women seemed so desperate to bleach their skins white, where television programmes were full of British and American shows. It seemed to her that the Ghanaian president was trying to project an *African personality* against monumental odds.

Personally for her, it was a slow adjustment that never finished its cycle, leaving open a loop that would never be closed. It was that elusive search for acceptance, an acceptance she wouldn't admit she wanted. But because she was admired for being American, because she saw the turn away from things African, she felt rejected in an odd way. She had thought her African-ness was what would win her admiration, not the American-ness, which she would have liked to see rejected, just as much as she would have liked to reject it. Inevitably, the two-pronged response of her Ghanaian counterparts irked her. There was the envy – her accent and the way she carried the English language, her straight hair (inherited in part from the legacy of slavery and its implants of white seeds in her ancestry), her seemingly easy access to money, her otherness – all combining into admiration. She could see it in the way they swarmed to her, wanting to be with her, to be like her, prodding her about life in America, asking her to take them with her when she returned. *Do you know what it is like to be black in America*? She wondered silently at the interest expressed by these newly independent people. Then there was the undercurrent of something that was at worst a benign dislike. Why couldn't she be more like them: the unequivocal deference to authority, for example; the way she spoke with her teachers (as if she was their coequal) and the slack they gave her because she was from somewhere else; the way she drove a car around like an adult; the way the boys were drawn to her...

It was better when she went to the University of Ghana, where the students were more mature. But still, her alienation continued. Was she being too sensitive? Why was she having that reaction? Why couldn't she just ride with the tide like her father seemed to be doing? When he married Sissi, she found someone from whom she could seek help. This was her mother. She was family. Fiona loved her, despite her earlier misgivings – not of dislike, but of suspicion that Sissi would be replacing her blood mother (but that suspicion dissolved when Sissi treated Fiona more as a sister than as a daughter). Sissi's empathy seemed striking. But at her age, Fiona was set in her ways. This was no time for changing and because Sissi was Ghanaian, the anchor she offered to help Fiona cope was still alien in many ways to Fiona and so the anchor lay fragile and uncertain.

So when her father decided to leave Ghana and return to the US, Fiona was excited. She did not hate the country where she'd finished her degree, started work (Ghana Commercial Bank), found a mother and found a sister soon to be born. It was like leaving the presence of an unfamiliar grandmother, hardly seen, not known, hardly missed. But, when she arrived in the US, she developed a slight dislike for Ghana, for she had acquired a little hint of a Ghanaian accent, difficult to shake off the taste of Ghanaian syntax. After she arrived in the US, she was prepared to reacquire her Americanness. To her, that was the surest way to succeed in a country that had little taste for other things coloured and alien. Coloured and alien – double whammy?

Thirteen

The time passed quickly as I wanted it to. So much had happened that I wanted to get away from while so much seemed to beckon in the future. Naturally, I was drawn to the latter, a hope that could still shimmer from the distance of tomorrow. I refocused on my studies and got almost all As. I anchored the educational with the emotional, getting closer to Fiona. We spent more time together and we got closer still, although our relationship was slightly tempered by our various obligations: she with work and I with studies.

During campus recruiting by corporations the fall before graduation, I signed up for several interviews but never got a job offer. I was aghast. What was happening? Why couldn't I get a job when all around me my friends were receiving many offers? Why, when my grades were better than at least eighty per cent of the class? Fiona would play me Aretha Franklin's *Respect*, asking that I take a cue from it. Ed and I watched *Super Bowl I* on CBS; he proclaimed that it was a great day for American football. But I could scarcely dwell on this as graduation soon descended on us that spring. I had no idea what I'd do, jobless as I was. John had been accepted to The Law School in Cambridge – a fact he never failed to celebrate before us, as if to taunt us. Dwayne was set to work for a bank in Detroit, an offer he received after long, painful interviews, he told me. On the strength of his father's recommendation, Ed had a job with an insurance company in Boston. Ed's choice was a surprise. I'd never expected he'd enter the corporate world. I'd expected him to enter the Peace Corps, do something for a socially conscious not-for-profit organization, or otherwise devote his youthful vigour in the service of some political movement for the underprivileged. There could be only one influence in this evolution: Jenny Arnold.

Considering the presence of others' parents, I would have loved to see my family at graduation, but it was an unrealistic wish, given the cost. I couldn't even afford one ticket. The only one who attended on my behalf was Fiona. She tried hard to fill the vacuum, buying me a congratulatory card and dinner. John got a car as his graduation present and Ed received a down payment on a house. Dwayne and I envied them. Neither of us got anything. "Someday I will give my kids something like these white boys get," Dwayne said, expressing the wish for the both of us. As it was, I went through graduation without much confidence, partly because I had no job offers and partly because I owed The University. I'd gone to see my financial aid adviser for more loans to cover the shortfall, but he said it was too late. I appealed to the Dean of Students, my old *friend*. Professor Redford said there was little he could do about it. As if to comfort me, he invited me over for dinner. If nothing at all, I was proud I'd conquered the fear of crossing the bridge in front of his house. That may have been the only consolation he could offer. "Don't worry, Jojo," he said, "you can still march with your classmates. You just won't get your diploma until you pay your bill. After graduation, just get a job and there'll be no problem." Easily said. Not easily done.

I did march with my classmates. Most displayed their diplomas proudly to cheering parents and siblings and friends. I too walked up to the podium when my name was mentioned and shook the president's hand. Then William Redford handed me a piece of paper the size of The University diploma. In the middle of the blank paper were written the words: Your diploma will be released to you after you fulfill your financial obligations to The University. I quickly folded the paper. I heard Fiona cheering me in the distance. I was bored and didn't listen to the speeches that followed. I was thinking instead about the future. My future.

After graduation, I moved off-campus to a small studio apartment. What was I to do with a degree in economics and no job nor prospects of one? Everywhere I went, I felt as if I was some sort of caricature set out to be humiliated, as though I were a panhandler to be shunned. Additional interviews (and I had many) all proved barren. It was a long struggle that I didn't know how to manage. I would leave in the early hours and go in search of jobs, my only suit neatly pressed, my hair combed to perfection. I would come home with creases in my suit, stale sweat in my shirts and besieged by depression. I would wash and iron the suit at night for the next day's adventures. It wasn't what I wished. I fought, but sometimes fights are lost despite the determination in the struggle. Then one day I went to the law offices of Rich & Swift downtown and knocked on the door, desperately hoping. I knew Winnie Redford used to work there. The receptionist looked up at me over the rim of her glasses. "May I help you?"

I didn't know what to say, but I wouldn't yield to the defeat and desperation that loomed. "May I see Mr. Swift, please?"

She refocused on me as though I were insane. "Mr. Swift?"

"Yes, madam."

She let elapse a confused pause. It wasn't a pregnant pause, for that implies something full; this was a negation, a hint of something lacking. "Mr. Swift died a month ago."

Wrestled off this gamble, I had few shots left, but I tried to fire them deftly. "My condolences, madam. How about Mr. Rich?"

"Do you have an appointment?"

"I don't with Mr. Rich, but I had met Mr. Swift some time back. I told him I was interested in the law and would appreciate the opportunity to work as a clerk for him. He said to come see him after I graduated and he would get me a job as a law clerk, so here I am." That was a sad lie, but I was desperate. I regretted that I'd not noticed his death. I was a bit ashamed for having tried to take advantage of this memory. I remembered the rally he organised that I'd attended with Phoebe.

"I see," said the receptionist. "Well, as you can see, it will be impossible to see him now."

"Yes, but perhaps I can see Mr. Rich?" I used my last card, hoping it would work. "Mrs. Winnie Redford spoke highly of him. She told me a long time ago before she passed that I could come talk to him."

"Winnie? You knew Winnie Redford?" She looked at me for long, hard seconds. "Wait here."

Oh, Jojo, what wretched exploitation of the dead. Shame. Shame. Shame.

The receptionist returned and led me to the office of Jonathan Rich, a small man, whose loudness seemed ample compensation for a diminished physical stature, his smile, louder than his grip, awed me in its wideness. He listened to me, his smile intact as if it was a permanent facial feature. "You just graduated from The University? Wonderful. Wonderful. It always impresses me when you Negroes manage it, you know. There aren't many of you in academic houses. And where do you say you're from? Ghana. Africa. Well, I'll be damned." He read the resume I'd given him seconds earlier. "You've done well for yourself, my boy." He'd be glad to give me a job, on a temporary, part-time basis, of course. I could help with some errands and perhaps learn one thing or two, he said. "Can't promise anything permanent right now. Let's see how it works out." But then the problem: he inquired and found out that I had no work papers. "Sorry, my boy, I'm a man of the law, need to do it all by the book. You go get your work papers and I'll be glad to give you a job." Couldn't he hire me and sponsor me for permanent residence? "No, can't do," he said.

That was it. I knew that if this continued any longer, I would be in dire circumstances. What was I to do? The rent was coming due. Without it I would be homeless. Desperate measures were needed. I went to The University job bulletin board and wrote down all the job listings without discrimination. Then I started calling. Even the menial jobs seemed out of reach. I'd talk for a minute and then receive the *Sorry* that came as a response. There was only one job left: stacking hay. I called. "Sure need help. Got a lot o' hay to stack, partner. You got a ride?"

"No."

"Okay, show me where you're at. I'll come pick you up in my pickup. Get it? Pick you up. Pickup? Ha ha ha." Was that a joke? I had to laugh too. He was my new boss.

Joe Wood picked me up as promised. He was a husky man with a long belly that signified strength rather than privilege. His labrador in the middle, I sat in the front of the pickup on the bumpy ride to the hay firm. The grass was already cut and bundled. We had to stack it in the barn. It was hard work, but because I needed the money desperately, I was grateful to have it, although I felt like a man forced to stay content with the discarded jetsam while the ship full of silver and gold floated away with only a select few aboard. It was hot in the barn, but not that bad to begin with. Joe would load the bundled hay from the farm, drive them over to the barn, drop them and then I'd start stacking. After he'd dumped enough he'd help me with the stacking, then we'd return to loading and unloading and stacking. We started at the back of the barn and worked towards the door in front. By midday, it was extremely hot in the barn, especially as I got to the top of the pile – we would stack about five layers and then pile them up to the very top, very close to the ceiling. It was like a furnace near the ceiling. We started at 8:30 am, took a lunch break at noon at a nearby deli and returned to work until 4:30 pm. Joe drove me back home and by then I would be tired (with aching muscles and a headache) and covered with dry sweat and the remnants of hay. When I would speak with Fiona, she'd insist I speak louder. "You have a booming voice, but you seem to be speaking softer and softer." I hadn't noticed. Was it possible that my voice had softened without my realizing it? Fiona was furious when she found out I was stacking hay. I wasn't sure whether it was at me for taking the job or generally because it seemed the only job available to me.

We saw each other more and more. I sacrificed my independence for a bit of her company. Ours had been, of sorts, an attraction at first sight, but it was an attraction initially carried more by the spiritual connection of the commonalities in our background. The physical would come later on that day in her room when blood brought us together. But was I ready to wed her and promise to love her until death parted us? I was close to that decision, but I took my time now that I was out of school. I needed certainty, still. It took me two months after graduation to believe we had a future together.

I did it the American way, borrowing money from Dwayne (who bemoaned the assassination of Martin Luther King, Jr. and lamented that America was going to hell) and a little from Ed (who would later call and lament the assassination of Robert Kennedy and assert that America was going to hell). I agreed for different reasons: I was in my own hell. But I was hoping to make it less hellish by marrying Fiona. I invited her to what I believed to be the most romantic restaurant in town: The Town Tavern. I was nervous and sweaty. If she rejected me, I would be lost forever in hopelessness. She had become a part of my emotional and spiritual compass, a guide of sorts. I got down on one knee after several gulps of cheap wine and asked her to marry me with the engagement ring held out to her. I felt a bit bad about it, as if it were a bribe. Vulnerable in my genuflection, I watched her shiver with excitement as tears fell, seeming to shimmer down her face, with the window's backdrop of night, a skyline of simplicity (of nothing but that night we'd walked in, the trees, the buildings, the dotted bright objects in the sky). Fiona agreed to marry me, while I wondered what hearts were breaking at that moment since just about every marriage stands on the hearts of those who were not chosen. I knew who mine was, but what of hers?

It was only later in the marriage, when we were both assured of each other, that she revealed to me her thoughts on the eve of our marriage:

God, I never thought I'd marry an African. Am I my father's daughter, after all? Or perhaps my mother's daughter? Going back to the heart of Africa for a husband. What will others say? My friends? That I couldn't find one of my own? Aren't there many Afro-Americans who'd do just fine? Take Marvin, for example, whom I'd so foolishly loved in high school and then dumped when Dave came along. Dave with his big talk about how big he was going to get. I can't believe I fell for that nonsense. That brother was just too antiseptic for my tastes. And then when we broke up . . . the way I longed for Marvin, thinking what a fool I'd been. And then there's Dennis, my first when I was only thirteen. What a sweet boy he was then, a year older, both of us so anxious . . . and then Kwame when I was in Ghana. Come to think of it, that was a drought . . . Ghana. Only one. And now Jojo. Not as fine as Marvin, or Dave, or even Dennis. But looks don't matter that much, do they? And he talks kind of funny – like Ma. But who cares how funny he talks? He makes me laugh; he's not bad in bed. And I love him. What more can I ask for?

As much as I didn't like her view at that time of my looks as compared to Marvin and the others, or of my accent, or of her apprehensions, I appreciated her honesty and her assertion of love.

I moved into Fiona's slightly larger apartment. Marrying her and moving into her apartment was not just to fulfill an emotional (or even spiritual) desire. It had a practical purpose, too. Marrying her would grant me permanent residence. It would be issued if we stayed married until Immigration made its final decision. If we divorced, my application would be rejected. Reduced to its crudest minimum, she held the power of returning me to Ghana at a time when I couldn't return. How could I return broke? What would I tell my family? I had come to America to stack hay? Under the circumstances, I developed a mild fear of Fiona. Perhaps I should rephrase that. It really wasn't fear, rather something akin to apprehension, something approximating a concern that crippled my ability to stand up to her, negated whatever leverage I might have had as her husband. I was afraid to argue with her too forcefully, press a point too far. If she insisted, I acquiesced. I rationalised my weakness. It would only be a short time. I'd get permanent residency and then I would neutralise her power. But the dynamics of marriage were being set, its foundation being built – and I would come to realise that when the foundation was firmly set, it would be almost impossible to build a house other than the one that suited the foundation; impossible to find a different tree apart from the roots that gave it life.

Amid this tentativeness, I learned she was pregnant – one of the happiest bits of news ever. While others applauded Neil Armstrong's walk on the moon and some marched in an anti-war rally in Washington DC, I watched Fiona's belly rise slowly with the months, dealt with her pre-partum tantrums and many moments of joy at the prospect of being a mother. I rubbed her belly and felt the baby kick and loved Fiona more. Against all of Fiona's protestations, I refused to be in the delivery room. I had my reasons. I couldn't imagine ever making love to Fiona again if I saw her give birth live with all its attendant complications. How could I not be turned off sexually after all that? Kudos to the men who are able to do it. Not me. Fiona acquiesced when I presented it that way. I stayed outside and waited for the news and then I went to the room.

I'd heard others joyous over their newborns, in fact I had myself often felt that thrill of seeing a new life, but nothing – I mean NOTHING – prepared me for the emotional avalanche that rode over me when Ama was born. She was like an extension of myself, but perfect. I swear I could have died for her there and then without a second thought if the bargain was offered. When it exists, love between husband and wife is intense, but the love between parent and child is indescribable, transcending transcendence itself. What a heavenly creation and what helpless reliance that made me love her even more – love taken to the limit and then the limit redefined to take it farther, and again and again until it becomes genuinely infinite and longer than time. (Not to say that Juju's birth wasn't important. But the first time always has a special significance.) All this love was tempered though – and I admit shamefacedly – by nipple envy: that the child now sucked on the nipples that the father used to suck on, the father watching what joy this seemed to bring the mother. Had it been the same joy as it had brought the wife?

Naming Ama was simple. Fiona had protested little and agreed when I suggested that she be named in the customary way in Ghana after the day she was born. For a Saturday born girl, it would follow that we'd name her Ama. Ama Badu, a beautiful name. Ed sent me a congratulatory card, William Redford sent me a bottle of champagne and Dwayne mailed me a gift certificate to a store for babies' clothes and toys.

I had the regret of leaving Ama to go to work and worse yet, work that I considered not befitting of her. I could reconcile myself to failure, but I couldn't reconcile myself to failing her. It was a difficult arrangement, but Fiona took some time off from work to help raise Ama. It was a mighty help when Sissi came over to stay with us. I had never felt so little. With my mother-in-law in the apartment, I was ashamed to go stack hay and return covered with it in the evenings. She said nothing. It wasn't her style, but I suspected she was dissatisfied. (Even on maternity leave, Fiona still brought in the bulk of our growing family's income.) Fiona encouraged me to apply for American citizenship. "If nothing at all, it might open new job opportunities for you. I was reluctant to apply, still holding on to a quickly fading belief that I'd return to Ghana, a belief that abided despite my resolve to make America my home after Uncle Kusi's death. Even if I didn't return, it seemed like the only – believe it or not – tangible connection I had to Ghana at that time. But after Fiona insisted, I applied for it and became an American citizen. The day I surrendered my Ghana passport, I felt as if I had killed a part of my identity and acquired a new one. I wept.

Phoebe called me. I hadn't spoken with her in a long while, not since graduation. I'd almost forgotten about her. Fiona picked the phone, rolled her eyes and said as she handed it over, "It's your white girlfriend." Phoebe's voice was beaming with enthusiasm. "Wow!" she said on learning we'd just had a baby. "That's way out, man." She told me she'd been involved in the Stop the Draft movement and then joined the National Organization of Women. "Needed to make something important out of all this mess," she said. "Tried to shake things up a bit. But then I got a bit tired, you know. Needed a bit of a break. So I quit and travelled Europe a while. Been back a year, you know... waiting tables. I've got to decide what to do now."

After I told her my story since graduation, a bit reluctantly, Phoebe exclaimed, "That's wild! How about getting out of there for a while? Me and some friends are going to the Woodstock Music and Arts Fair in upstate New York next month. We're leasing a farmhouse up there, if you want to join us. You, Fiona and the baby."

I'd heard about the festival, but hadn't given it much thought. "I can't Phoebe," I said. "Not with the baby and all."

"Well, if you change your mind, let me know."

She called again after the festival. "Jojo, you missed out, man." She told me how their party of six went to Bethel, New York for the festival. "It was the biggest gathering of people for peace and love. Even with the rain and mud, it was wonderful. We were mud sliding down a hill and high as hell. Just rad, man... strangers offering their blankets, offering pot and other stuff... Vietnam vets, positive people all over. Man, there was lots of positive feeling. And, oh, the music was far out... Grateful Dead, Arlo Guthrie, Jimi Hendrix, Ravi Shanker, The Who, Santana, Janis Joplin... Jojo, I hardly slept for three days but I felt wide awake, high on the energy."

I could only imagine. I'd seen parts of it on television and heard a comment that the crowd reached about 400 thousand. I could imagine Phoebe with the two finger V sign for peace, her long hair wet from rainfall, her eyes glazed from marijuana, swaying her hips, saying something to a stranger about universal love, blasting the Vietnam War and the US's involvement in it, heading somewhere to have sex with some stranger. I envied her more than she knew – the fearlessness, the freedom, the free spiritedness. I wished I could have some of that. But I had more immediate concerns: Fiona, Ama and a future to find, which at that moment seemed bleak. As I replayed Phoebe's presence at Woodstock, compared all that she'd done since graduation, I felt trapped for the first time since I'd known Fiona. I needed to do something and it had to be done soon; otherwise, I feared what might happen to us.

So something had to change. I couldn't continue to let Fiona bear me on her meagre earnings, not after Ama was born. Nor could I continue to work stacking hay. I needed ideas. When I spoke with Dwayne next, he impressed on me an option. "I'm applying to law school," he said.

"Law school? You're the last person I'd have thought would want to go to law school."

"Times change, brother. I'm tired of working at the bank, getting nowhere."

"And what are you going to do with a law degree?"

"We'll see. I may be able to do a lot more good for the cause."

He got me thinking. I was way past thinking about any *cause* except my own. Couldn't I too go to law school? Hadn't I done well in college, well enough that I was at the top twenty percentile of my graduating class? Why shouldn't I be able to handle the law? Plus, most of the lawyers I knew, including my father-in-law, seemed successful (and success at that time meant financially comfortable). I became all the more interested the more I considered it. It had to help ease my current drab situation. "What say you that I try law school?" I asked Fiona.

"Why not? You'll make a good lawyer. I've actually thought about going myself."

"Are you serious?"

"Yeah, I might do it someday."

Might do it someday was all I needed. If I was going to law school, I couldn't wait for Fiona to beat me to it. She was beating me to many things and had already established herself as *de facto* head of the household. I knew law school meant three more years of depending on her, but I saw little choice. The next day, I borrowed books from the local library and started reading about law schools. Within a month I was formally applying to law school.

It was a tedious application process: studying for and taking the Law School Admission Test (LSAT), writing a personal statement, getting recommendations (one of which I got from William Redford), filling out the application form and paying the application fees (which Fiona did). Studying for the LSAT was a particular challenge. With a baby and a wife and briefly, a mother-in-law, I had to struggle to find time and space. I considered quitting. The hell with everything, I would say. It was only my dedication to make a better life for Ama that guided me through. I spent long nights in the library, though tired from all the familial and work duties. I would listen to Simon & Garfunkel's *Bridge Over Troubled Water* over and again, for inspiration, which was at best tenuous. Ed called me not long after I decided to apply. He was applying too. I wasn't surprised. He had the ability and disposition, especially his way with people. He was taking a professional preparation course for the LSAT. I'd have liked to take that course too, but the fees were way out of my budget. I had to rely on my native skill and intelligence. I hardly had any sleep the night before the exam. Apart from the natural anxiety that promotes sleeplessness, there seemed to be an ongoing party not too far from us that woke me up several times during my short sleeping hours. When I walked into the exam room, I was numb from fatigue, sustained by only two cups of coffee. I managed to get into the seventy-fifth percentile, Ed was in the ninety-fifth.

Now I could only wait for the results of my applications. It too was a torment of sorts. I had convinced myself that getting into law school would be the panacea to all my financial woes, the elixir for my growing self-doubt, loss of self-respect and its attendant lack of confidence. Therefore, I viewed each envelope in the mailbox with hope and trepidation. My fate, in my mind, rested with the eight schools to which I applied. By now, Sissi had returned to DC and Fiona, Ama and I waited.

The first two responses were rejections. They were from the lesser renowned schools from the lot. That depressed me deeply, especially when Dwayne called to tell me he'd been accepted to The Law School. I was mightily jealous, even though I was glad for him. He said something about being set for the rest of his life. My own concerns could have drowned his elation if they could drip water. I felt incapacitated, more trapped than ever, wearied by an inertia that I feared might never end.

Would I forever stack hay? That night, Fiona did for me what loving spouses do. She tried to cheer me, but realizing her efforts were inadequate under the circumstances, she made love to me like it was the first time. The (joyful) stress of Ama in the household and the strains of our jobs had held our sex life hostage. But that night, led by Fiona, we would elude the hijackers . . . she invited me into the bath with her and washed me down, ever so slowly. She was still attractive, Fiona. Her belly was still a bit extended from the pregnancy (although she'd been exercising to flatten it again) and her breasts were beginning to sag (although still full with breast milk) but all that didn't matter. She led the way and when I tried to intervene, she wouldn't let me. "This is for you, honey . . . " Our lovemaking that night was ecstatic. I felt rejuvenated the next day, revived by the knowledge of Fiona's love and the existence of Ama who was a multiplication of that love and mine.

That evening a large manila envelope arrived with The Law School's logo embossed on the front. I shook as I opened it and then when I saw the word "Congratulations . . . " I screamed and threw the letter at Fiona. In the next second, she was hugging me, kissing me, teary-eyed, saying, "I'm so proud of you." I did an awkward pirouette, fell on my knees in the living room and yelled, "Thank you, God!"

I called Dwayne immediately. "It will be like old times again," he said. "I can't wait."

I called Ed next. "Hey, man, I just got in . . . "

"Where?"

"The Law School."

"Oh how wonderful! You must be so excited."

"You can't imagine. Have you heard yet?

"Not yet. I'm still waiting."

"Don't worry, you'll get in."

"I hope so," he said, "but hey, I'm not from Africa or anything, you know. I'm competing against a different pool."

The rest of our conversation lost its meaning. Somehow – and I know without ill intent – his words deflated my buoyancy: *I'm not from Africa or anything, you know*. Fiona told me not to dwell on it and I tried, but occasionally it would creep back into my mind... *I'm not from Africa or anything*... I got into The Law School because I'm African? Three days later, Ed called to tell me he'd been accepted. As I thought about it I realised how bizarre it was, but the circle was indeed complete: Dwayne, Ed and I all headed for The Law School. And to think of it, John was already there.

I stood on The University Park for a long time and waited for the large clock in the library's tower to chime; I walked over Professor Redford's bridge to bid him farewell and hear him state his pride in me; I walked down Frat Row, remembering the many nights of insane alcohol consumption; I spent a few minutes in the woods and at The University Pond, watching the trees and the pond they encircled – I'd been afraid to go there often because of the way they drew me in, seeming to promise a tranquility that I knew I couldn't sustain.

Fiona, Ama and I moved to Cambridge that fall. Fiona quit her job at The University. I'd said she didn't have to – we could visit each other as often as was necessary. After all, it was only a few hours away. But she didn't want that distance. "What? Leave you to those law schoolgirls? No way." She applied for a number of job openings at colleges in Boston and got one in the Cambridge area. We found a small apartment in Cambridge, within walking distance for both of us. Ama was still growing and such a delight – perhaps even more so than before.

The next day, we went to Ed and Jenny's wedding. It was a lush ceremony, to be succinct. Mark and Anne Palmer financed the church ceremony, which had no less than a hundred guests. My understanding was that Jenny's parents bankrolled the evening reception: abundant drinks and multi-coursed dinner in a chandeliered ballroom at an exclusive country club where even the air seemed tasteful and acquired at great expense. "I couldn't have had it better," Ed said to me. "I'm so ready to face law school," he added. I understood what he meant by that. He must have been affirming his faith in Jenny and the belief that with a woman such as her as his support, there was nothing that could faze him. I felt that way as well. How could I go wrong with Fiona and Ama?

But not so fast. Nothing had or could have prepared me for The Law School. The first few days were mostly for orientation – filled with speeches, including the Dean's welcoming remarks about hard work, the Black Law Students Association organizing symposia to help black students cope and succeed, an orientation group of seven first year students (or 1Ls) led by a third year (or 3L) who gave advice most of which I forgot. And then there were the unavoidable parties, which I didn't attend because I had to be with Ama and Fiona. Our orientation team leader showed us where to buy books and pick up our assignments for the first day of class. I'd taken a huge loan from The Law School, so I didn't have to worry about financial matters (until later when the loans would come due and I had to repay). I repaid my debts to Dwayne, Ed and the short-term debt to The University (with the loans to be repaid later).

When all was over, I started to prepare for the next day's class. I should have started earlier. I'd never read a law case in my life. The diction was obscure, the reasoning convoluted. Sometimes I had to read cases again and again and still couldn't quite comprehend the meaning of their inscrutable sentences. Did some of these judges simply want to make a law student's life miserable? I wondered. I thought I'd mastered the English language appreciably well, but this was something else. It was a new language: the language of the law. Plus Latin phrases dotted the cases like road bumps, the meanings for which I had to keep looking up in my law dictionary. By ten o'clock, I'd finished only one assignment out of three classes for the next day. Luckily, Torts was the first class. I read the Contracts assignment next and decided to do the Civil Procedure reading between classes the next day. It was two o'clock when I went to bed, three-quarters asleep already. I woke up at five, one-quarter awake, read through my notes for Torts and Contracts and headed for my eight o'clock class. I sat in the seat assigned me for the semester, introduced myself to my neighbours and waited.

A bearded Professor James walked into class with textbooks in one arm and a seating chart in the other. From my seat, I could see the chart had our pictures pasted to our seating arrangements. The professor set his books on the desk, opened one of them and looked at the seating chart. There was a silence that cut sharply with the unspoken question: Who will be the first to be called on? I remembered Mburu's words years earlier: *Here, you represent all of Africa, all of the black race. They are watching you. Remember that, whatever you do.* I prayed for the cup to pass. It didn't.

"Mr. Badu," Professor James said, "Would you state the case of..."

I'm not sure I heard him. Had he, of all the hundred students in the class, called my name? What was it about Jojo Badu that made him do so? Couldn't he call someone with a more familiar name like Bond or Johnson? I could feel my heart pumping, sweat spreading, stomach clenching. I wasn't sure I could speak. "Umm..." I said. "The case, sir?"

"Yes, that's what I said. Would you state it?"

"Which case, sir?"

"Mr. Badu, you just heard me state the name of the case. Or was I talking to the wind?"

"I'm sorry..."

"Sorry? When you appear before a judge, you don't want to be sorry. Your client's case, a life, could depend on it." Professor James returned to his chart. "Mr. Green, will you tell us the name of the case?"

Mr. Green dutifully stated it.

"Thank you, Mr. Green. Now, Mr. Badu, will you state the case for us?"

It was the first case in the textbook. I had read it, briefed and reread it. That very morning, I'd read my notes. I knew it. But with my body so tense, Mburu's advice replaying in my mind, about a hundred of my colleagues staring at me, my mind went blank. I tried to remember the facts, the arguments, the reasoning, the ruling...but still NOTHING, except certain disjointed phrases. "We are waiting, Mr. Badu."

"I'm sorry, sir, I can't remember the case."

"You can't remember or you didn't read it?"

"I read it, Professor James. I... I can't recall it."

"Mr. Badu," he sighed heavily. "Preparation is essential for a successful law school career as it is for a successful legal career." He turned to face the class. "I don't want Mr. Badu's example to be the standard. Now, Mr. Green, will you state the case for us?"

The rest of class was a blur. Humiliation would be an understatement. I couldn't think. Contracts wasn't as dramatic for me, but I didn't have the calmness of mind to read for Civil Procedure. Luckily, I wasn't called on in either class (and I particularly liked the friendliness of the Civil Procedure teacher). I was walking home in shame when I saw John Owens, then a 2L. He knew I was coming, he said. He'd seen my name on the list of the first year students. He seemed more at ease than in college, calmer. I told him of my humiliation. "Don't worry about it," he said. "It happens to the best of us. You can't let that sort of thing get to you."

"It was so embarrassing."

"What? That you couldn't answer a professor's questions? It's really no big deal, trust me."

But... *Here, you represent all of Africa, all of the black race.*

I learned that John was on Law Review and wrote for the campus newspaper, *The Law Record*, which was generally mainstream.

Whatever happened that morning, I was determined not to let it happen to me again. I told Fiona I was going to have to work harder than I thought. I spent most of my afternoons in the library and went home late. I'd return to campus after dinner and spend countless hours late into the night studying (because it was difficult to study at home). Time ceased to matter (or, rather, perhaps it mattered too much because I didn't have enough of it). I didn't have any to spare so there was no need keeping track. I tried to spend time with Fiona and Ama, but I just couldn't afford much with them. Much as I tried, I often fell behind in my class assignments and I was always striving to catch up. I got called on in Professor Janet O'Grady's Civil Procedure and managed to hold my own, even though the apprehension abided. I never got called on in Torts again (presumably because Professor James was disappointed with my performance the first time). I did okay the first time I was called on in Contracts, but the second time I'd stayed up almost all night and could barely stay coherent.

Generally, I felt I'd lost control. I didn't get enough sleep, was stressed by the tedium of class and pressured by the demands of family life. Fiona didn't complain and in those brief sane times, I admired her for that. Once I felt stressed beyond limit and mentioned to Fiona I wanted to quit. "I have every faith in you," she said. "Hang in there." I did. I saw Ed and Dwayne from time to time, but none of us had time to gallivant or do much chit-chatting.

Fall had cooled and drawn in the winter when the first semester ended. We would have a Christmas break and begin exams in January, which meant I'd spend all of the holidays studying – not the best prescription for family happiness. This time, Fiona was upset that I spent so much time in the library. But she didn't fret much. The exams, however, seemed anti-climatic. Three hours each of long fact patterns and complicated questions, but not as difficult as I'd feared. I ended up with a B+, B+ and B. Not stellar, but decent.

The second semester was more of the same. Having survived one semester, however, I was beginning to understand the new language I was studying. I could get through assignments quicker and see a bit more of Fiona and Ama. I was able to see Dwayne and Ed a bit more too. And occasionally I'd run into John. He invited me to his apartment for beer (as he had done once or twice in college). I noticed he still had his unicorn painting, which he continued to adjust; still seeking that it hung perfectly, it seemed.

That spring, I did several interviews with the hope of a summer internship at a law firm. "It helps build your experience, which is what the law firms will be looking for," John explained.

After twenty interviews, I had no offers. "I thought being at The Law School would open doors for you," Fiona said.

"So did I."

I still didn't have a summer internship when I started my second semester's exams (Corporations, Property and Criminal Law). Panicked, I asked The Law School Career Counseling Services for help. They referred me to the Public Interest Director who managed to place me with a Public Interest Committee in downtown Boston, a not-for-profit criminal defense organization that paid nothing. I had to rely on a miserly stipend from The Law School. Fiona continued to bear the bulk of the financial responsibilities. It was difficult, but we were hopeful of future prospects. The summer job was a bit of a blessing, however. The hours were as I chose them. No one paid much attention to what I did: basic research and memo writing, accompanying lawyers to court on occasion and generally just looking interested. Given the flexibility, I had a bit more time to spend with Fiona and Ama and they both loved it as I did. We ate breakfast together and took walks in the evenings and Fiona and I made love more frequently. In a way, I fell in love again. In the meantime, Dwayne was working for a small law firm in DC, Ed was working for a major law firm in Los Angeles and John was doing the same in DC. My grades were better that semester: B+, B+, A-. Not bad at all. I looked forward to my second year. I had a wonderful family. And I had friends.

Fourteen

But the second year of law school would test us. In the middle of that winter a fire was lit on campus and raged as if with licentious lust. That was when the *event* happened and we would become four students in a unique alliance: three Americans and one African, in some ways feeling abandoned like jetsam jettisoned to drown in a cresting sea. It would not end for a long, singed season (or so it seemed to me) during which lives would intersect, align and emerge irretrievably altered: like my own many lives, more magical than a cat's famed nine lives, more numerous. I too had died several times and each time I'd found the power within to grow another life – as I had to; there was no other choice. (The mosaic of our colours must have added some intrigue to onlookers. In those days I still struggled not to think in terms of skin shades, but time and again I couldn't escape it.) There was no magic to it though, just the instinct to survive. But each time I died and lived, the death and resurrection left me with an altered soul, not necessarily better or worse, just different; sometimes stronger, sometimes weaker. That particular night in my second year of law school, however, I wasn't contemplating my own will and how it would emerge from the latest death. I knew I would live again as I had mustered the power of resurrection little by little until it became second nature: as natural as my own breath. My concern was what kind of life would emerge.

For a moment, I cast a quick look outside to the falling soft sheet of snow. While the fire raged on, I stood there briefly in immobile thought as the snow continued to come and become what seemed to be a white wall of night. That I would marry the outside snow with the internal inferno momentarily stunned me, but there was no denying that the snow continued to fall and the fire continued to rage. And none of us knew how it would end. And our cause was neither accepted nor debunked, just not addressed.

It was an audacious act. I thought I could almost hear students whisper as they huddled in obscure spaces. "Outrageous!" They would say. "They could have protested." To that I would have answered, *Done that.* To "They could have organised a sit in," I would respond, *Done that.* They would suggest this (such as boycotting classes) and that (such as petitioning the president) and to each I would offer the same refrain: *Done that.* I knew I could never sufficiently explain why the usual means of student protest broke from its limits that day.

I hoped that the administration's decision, when it came, would be influenced by those sympathetic to the cause, who believed that it was more important than the rules that sought to regulate student protest. I asked myself: "What are those rules?" The rule of the institution: its laws to which every student must yield in order to glue the institution together, not just as a coherent whole, but as an acceptable smaller frame of the larger society. It had happened during college. Yannis. William Redford. I should have known... I knew. And so the rule: to threaten the microcosm was to threaten the whole. I knew then that I must, with telescopic vision, hold the institution The Law School as a mirror to the larger world it represented. Because I had been through it before in college, it appeared history was coming full circle but with some altered characters. Only this time I wasn't an agent after the fact, but in the middle of the protest itself.

As I watched the descending snow, I imagined the roar of those whose admiration I'd earned. Because they didn't have the fortitude to do what I'd done, they would offer their support if someone else did it. Yet, as I'd find out, it was one thing to have their support and another thing to translate that support into a frontal opposition to the full weight of authority.

But what disturbed me most was the group that would not take sides. "Big deal," they'd say, shrugging shoulders burdened with fat books as they only engaged the campus in singular pursuit of their diplomas. They would neither condemn nor praise, preferring the sanctified space of their neutrality. I was almost certain that within that group there were those who held great sympathy for the cause, but were closed within a circle either of apathy or complacency. In certain times, I could empathise with that attitude, but because at that moment I'd reached within myself and found the lever to leap forward, I had to believe that others could do so too.

I returned to the earlier night to retrieve what had just transpired in my room when our *Group of Four* had met to discuss its plight. It had been a solemn beginning constrained by what might be waiting in the future we all must have viewed with some fear – the prospect of expulsion. Expulsion! Had I come this far to be expelled over this?

"Why did you have to hit the Dean?" John had barked abruptly.

"Keep your voice low," I said. "Fiona and Ama are asleep."

"Stop picking on him," said Ed. "We're in this together."

"God, I hate this," John replied.

"Show some balls."

John chopped the air with frustrated fists. "If he hadn't hit the Dean, it wouldn't be a big deal. You realise that, don't you?"

Dwayne had stayed silent those slow minutes and listened. Reduced to its crux, both John and Ed acknowledged I shouldn't have struck the Dean, but they differed on assigning blame. John wagged the accusatory finger at me; Ed stood in the thicket of our collective venture to blame no one but rather to seek a solution to the recurring question: "What next?" For half an hour the two debated and cursed until I lost the logic of their argument, knowing that my face must have been a spectrum of emotions, now frowning, now relaxed, my hopes ebbing, my concern growing, turning into resignation and then growing into anger.

"We're getting nowhere," Dwayne finally said. "I'm out of here."

"Yeah," said John. "It's just like you to leave when we have to think over this problem, isn't it?"

"Look, I don't want any crap from you tonight, all right?" Because Dwayne blared such anger, his eyes narrowing, John made no reply.

Dwayne left us in the momentary silence his anger imposed. When he was gone, John began pacing the room. His quick pace sowed such anxiety in me I started pacing too. Ed couldn't bear the dual motion of John and

I and his fists came down heavily on a desk. "Stay still!" he yelled.

"Don't tell me what to do!" John countered.

And then my boiling frustration vented itself in such forceful words it sent spasms through the other two: "Shut up!" The terseness of the two words belied the strength bearing them. Ed sat silently and John stood frozen with balled fists. With a more relaxed mood I said, "I am the one most responsible for this. I am the one who hit him. I am the one who will bear the brunt of whatever is to come. If you can't do better than this, just leave me alone. I can't stand this bickering anymore."

Ed and John must have realised that the anger was directed inward as well as at them. They took the anger as giving their perspective cause and the prospect of punishment. They took it as a call to concert, an ill-defined search for the sense of community within them. And yet at that moment when I had captured their allegiance, even if for a few moments, I didn't capitalise on the mantle of leadership they briefly offered me; rather, I sunk down to what they'd all battled – confusion. It was a weakness that hindsight only magnifies. Wiping my face with both hands, I whispered, "Oh, what have I done? What am I going to do?"

"Let's not sweat this," said Ed. "Things will work out somehow. I have a gut feeling nothing's going to come out of this." Still, Ed's thoughts were throbbing for an escape from the gloomy prospect of expulsion. He too hadn't expected the assault on the Dean and yet after the fact he wasn't ready to repudiate it. He couldn't reject our plan and he could not now assign blame simply because what they hadn't anticipated had happened. If he were to rely on the expediency of hindsight, he might as well blame himself because he should have foretold the logical result of our acts, he reasoned.

"We'll see," John said. "I'm leaving."

"That guy's nuts," Ed said after John left. Then he asked me, "See you tomorrow?"

"Yes," I said without conviction.

"You'll be all right?" Ed asked.

"I'll be fine." Echoed words without conviction. There we were, two men within a vortex we couldn't control. Outside, the snow continued to collapse into snow; inside we looked at each other as if renewing our acquaintance, an African and an American attempting still (after so many years) to bridge oceans and histories as diverse as skin colour, or as irrelevant.

"Okay, catch you later," Ed said solemnly as though the moment was too heavy to bear.

I wished Ed would stay a little longer. Not that it would solve anything. Yet even a quiet presence would be more comforting than the prospect of mastering my fears solo. Fiona couldn't be a part of this. I wouldn't bring her into it yet. Briefly I confronted the fear washing over me, pulling me this way and that, vowing that through affirmations I'd have to remould my fear into something more positive. Still, I couldn't negate the sum of experiences that foretold something less benign than I hoped for. When I went and lay on my bed, Fiona was still asleep. I wished I could borrow her calm, but I was seized by the trouble I sensed was imminent: not the bedfellow I wished for at that slow hour. If only I'd not struck the Dean, it would be a protest and no more. The Law School had seen many of those. But assault and battery were another matter. I tried hard to find the reason for my act. Why? Why? Why? The question ran raucously and irritatingly. But the *Why* behind the deed couldn't be reduced to simple sentences nor made visible item after item like clothes on a line. It was more complicated, part of a larger picture – the assault was a trickle in an ocean, but the trickle was all others would allow themselves to see.

Plus the assault could have been something else – something worse. Or it might have not happened at all. Behind the dark curtains formed by my closed eyelids, I saw ghosts of dread and doom – a factory of fear with quadrupled output. The tightening in my groin stressed the urgency with which I viewed my potential fate.

Fifteen

Resolve: to mould inspiration, unhurriedly like the drops of sun-melted snow icicles from the rooftops. Dripping slowly. I imagined they would collect underneath into a puddle and then enlarge into something grander than the individual drips.

Morning had come. I gathered my books and stepped outside into the cold and encircling wind. I tried to pull up the zip on my jacket, but it was already fully zipped. I walked as leisurely as my unmasked fatigue. The night of haunting thoughts had left its strains. I'd stayed awake for hours in tormenting confusion like a man approaching lunacy.

The snow's sunny reflection hurt my bloodshot eyes as I walked quickly to class. I kept my head bowed in the hope that it would deter questions. But I couldn't escape the inevitable; only postpone it. Class was a nightmare to be forgotten. I couldn't concentrate as the predicament kept nagging me. And I dozed off once or twice. I thought I'd be prepared for the landslide of questions that came after class. In the anguished quiet of night, I'd prepared answers. Although I'd rather not speak to anyone, the questions found me as an arrow finds its target.

"What happened?"

"Is it really true?"

"What did you do?"

"Has the Dean said anything?"

It went on and on like a mistuned song, following me from classroom to corridors, from corridors to hallways and even to the vast outside. I responded in the skeletal hope that by voicing my answers, I could somehow find camaraderie and therefore, the strength they say resides in numbers. I kept my answers general because I didn't want to betray any solidarity between the *Group of Four* at the same time as I felt as if this was a deed with some sacred aspects that needed protecting. It was a perplexing thought to me that I would need such protectiveness. But perhaps that was precisely the point: that such actions needed a space of their own to thrive and evolve until they were ready to find voice. So I was polite but noncommittal, forthright, but not detailed. It was true, yes. The Dean hadn't said anything yet. And then I scurried away, not having quashed curiosity, but nourished it.

Fiona was supportive. "I'm here for you no matter what happens," she said. When her father called that evening, Fiona told him. George Harris asked to speak with me. "I want you to know how proud of you I am, son. It reminds me of that day in Ghana when Martin Luther King made his march on Washington." *Come now, old man, please don't stretch this that far.* He continued, "Who were we, but just American Negroes, as they used to say in those days. We were living in Ghana, but we had to find a way to support Martin. So a bunch of us gathered and marched on the US embassy in Accra. Son, it was the most exhilarating thing I'd done in a long time. And you know what's most interesting about it? DuBois died that same night. I had never felt so right about anything I'd done. I couldn't imagine how bad I'd have felt if I hadn't joined the march only to know that one of Africa's greatest men had died that very night. I would have died, too... Anyway, Jojo, I just wanted you to know how proud I am. Keep your spirits up, son." I suspected he'd concocted the story solely to strengthen me; still, his effort was uplifting.

Sixteen

So what occasioned this confrontation, this episode with the Dean of The Law School? It was part of a simple request into which poured a great deal and around which the forces arrayed were as powerful as they were entrenched. It would invoke memories of William Redford, my capitulation to him and it would invoke guilt I thought I'd overcome long ago. Like a walk into the depths of a night that has no visible horizons, this too would begin a difficult journey for me. At times, I felt as though I'd been stripped naked, standing vulnerable before my executioner's guillotine.

This thing had old roots, probably reaching back to my college years. Let me begin however with the more immediate prologue: a History of American Jurisprudence class I'd picked in my attempt to set the current culture of law in its historical context. That was my benign intention. Overall, the course was sufficiently enjoyable, teaching of various intellectual schools, their dialectics and the practical reactions to them from the staleness of historical lenses. That was the case until we reached one particular Supreme Court case: *Dredd Scott v. Sandford* (1857). Professor Paulson set the discussion in context, but his calmness was not consistent with the coming turmoil. Scott's master had taken him to the free part of the Louisiana territory where slavery was prohibited by virtue of the Missouri Compromise of 1820. After they returned to St. Louis, Missouri and after his master's death, Scott sued, arguing that since slavery was outlawed in the free Louisiana territory and he'd become free there, he remained free. Once free, now free. The Supreme Court of the United States of America ruled that a slave did not have the rights of a citizen to sue in federal court, because a slave was equivalent to property and couldn't be deemed a citizen. Chief Justice Taney's opinion stated in part:

> ...they were at that time considered as a subordinate and inferior class of beings, who had been subjugated by the dominant race and whether emancipated or not, yet remained subject to their authority and had no rights or privileges but such as those who held the power and the government might choose to grant them ...It is too clear for dispute, that the enslaved African race were not intended to be included and formed no part of the people who framed and adopted this declaration; for if the language, as understood in that day, would embrace them, the conduct of the distinguished men who framed the declaration of independence would have been utterly and flagrantly inconsistent with the principles they asserted; and instead of the sympathy of mankind, to which they so confidently appealed, they would have *deserved and received universal rebuke and reprobation*...
>
> (emphasis added)

Professor Paulson read the opinion almost in its entirety and I was negatively transfixed by it: subordinate and inferior... rather than sympathy of mankind... *deserved and received universal rebuke*... So, then, the African class of beings didn't belong in the stratum of humankind? If not, where did it belong? Listening to the opinion read, something terrible lodged inside me, something that wanted to lash out. It was as if every little slight, every misstated word was coagulating, congealing into something vile and ugly. Understood that it was an 1857 opinion, that it was met with considerable disgust, that it had been subsequently invalidated, yet that the opinion could be formulated in the first place by the highest court of the land was infuriating. I wondered if any or who among us – even my classmates – would consciously or unconsciously endorse the principles espoused in that opinion. If I had any guts, I would have stood on my desk and stepped foot and body on the opinion, literally and figuratively and expressed my infuriation. I would have voiced, nay vehemently vented, all the questions whirling through my mind. I might have held Professor Paulson by the neck and asked, "How can you read this outrageous opinion so calmly?" But, instead, I listened and got angry – an anger that festered inside, unexpressed.

It had continued the day Sithole came to lecture on campus. His was billed simply as a lecture by a South African exile about the political situation in South Africa. This wasn't unusual as The Law School had on occasion brought political speakers to the campus. But it was unusual in the sense that this was the first time a native born South African was invited to speak on a controversial matter. I would wonder why the school had done it. Had they no idea what fire he could light? Or was it their attempt to maintain a fair façade? After all, this was an institution of higher learning, where all shades of thinking were to be exposed and debated in the so-called marketplace of ideas. Perhaps it was a matter of simple miscalculation, an expectation that, indebted to the school for the invitation, he would skim the surface of an explosive issue and leave in the satisfaction of the invitation, thereby validating the school's purported openness to alternative points of view.

And, come to think of it, I hadn't even planned on attending. I'd gone because Dwayne insisted on it. I couldn't resist his persistent requests or justify a rejection. If Dwayne was so enthused about it, how dare I not be? I was African (as was Sithole), but Dwayne could only claim the African-ness through history or by hyphenation: Afro-American. Though, as it would turn out, Dwayne and Sithole had a lot more connecting them than I could lay claim to, a certain experience of tears and blood and suffering transcending the oceanic divide, the continental gulf. I had flown over that divide without paying attention to the ghosts that inhabited it, but which inevitably would come hunting for the ears and hearts of its progeny, regardless of their willingness or reluctance.

It was three o'clock when Sithole walked into the conference room, ready to address the relatively sparse audience of about twenty. Convinced by Dwayne of the speech's importance, I was disappointed with the low turnout. Sithole would otherwise be a nondescript figure, but it was evident that he was a man with a mission – focused, determined, perhaps not even dissuadable. I deduced these even before he started speaking. He'd entered the room with the briskness of a fervent storm, for the fervour seemed encapsulated inside him, in every step. As he stood behind the professor of international law who would introduce him, Sithole seemed to shake with an impatience wrestling him for control; after all, control was the pervasive attribute of the moment. Even I was beginning to grow impatient as the introducer droned on. I was impatient with anticipation, with the need to know what was bottled inside this almost dwarfish man with a giant's presence. When he finally took the lectern, Sithole grasped attention. He didn't have to ask that we lend him our ears; in fact, he owned them. That, needless to say, didn't surprise me. His voice wasn't booming, but it was poignant because it seemed magnified with passion and the approximately five-foot-five frame rose higher than the eyes beheld. If silence were a soldier, it would have saluted many times over and again.

"Thanks very much for coming . . . " he had begun, but it appeared he was in no hurry. He picked his words carefully, in contradiction to the passion that seemed to want to strike free.

"It is not always that one gets an audience of such intelligence and I am hoping, sympathy," he continued. "My name is Walter Sithole, born and raised in South Africa, now exiled because of my membership in the African National Congress. I can tell you of my own experiences in graphic detail, of the many times when I was denied access to basic things because I was the wrong colour, of the denial of basic decency because of the colour of my skin, of the discrimination that denies a man his humanity on the basis of his skin pigmentation. I could tell you these things as I have personally experienced them. But my personal story is a pale apparition of nothingness compared to some other atrocities inflicted on those in South Africa at large who have a dark hue, especially its black inhabitants. This, ladies and gentlemen, is a story of woe, a denial, mockery and suppression of humanity and a continuing dehydration of the wells of justice by the powers that believe it perfectly legitimate that one group, by distinction of different skin colour, has the birthright to deny others basic necessities, basic human rights.

"I will not take too much of your time by retracing the history of those of us native to a land who are denied access to the accoutrements of decent existence by those who have come from different lands. But, ladies and gentlemen, that is South Africa for you. It's past history tells much, but in the interest of time, let me begin in more recent times, specifically in 1948, when the National Party won elections under the banner of apartheid, a word that means simply *separateness*. Through a series of laws, the National Party has entrenched and intensified the horrific suppression of the black populace. I mention, as examples, the Population Registration Act of 1950, the Immorality Act, the Urban Labour Preference Policy, The Abolition of Passes and Documents Act, the Native Laws and Amendment Act, the Group Areas Act. Some of these laws and their related practices require all Africans to carry passbooks indicating employment history and residence. They prohibit a wide range of basic rights you take for granted, not least of which are freedoms of association, speech and let me say freedom to live as a human being. These, ladies and gentlemen are part of the *legal* apparatus that help enforce and wedge deep this diabolical system of separateness called apartheid.

"But let me not bore you any further with such legal umbrellas of oppression and injustice. I mention them only as a brief illustration of the deep-seated and conscious attempt to legitimise the illegitimate, to render legal that which is by any reasonable measure illegal. I stand before you today a humble representative of the oppressed. Let me tell you a little about how I came to leave South Africa. I promised you I'd keep this general and not personal, but I'm afraid I have to break my promise a little. Bear with me.

"In March of 1960, I was among a group of about 5,000 that gathered in Sharpeville in front of a police station. We had gathered in a simple demonstration against the apartheid system for, like Americans, we too believe in life, liberty and the pursuit of happiness. When the police tried unsuccessfully to disperse us with batons, they fired into the crowd, a crowd armed at best with stones. It was a run for dear life, ladies and gentlemen, in the pandemonium that followed the helter-skelter they forced on us. When you are faced with the threat of death, you acquire supernatural powers. I ran like a gazelle, faster than I thought possible. At one point, I saw a boy who couldn't have been more than fifteen go down, blood oozing from a body that must have been dying. If I were a bolder man, if I had any courage, I would have stopped at that moment to help that young man. As I ran, he cried out, with his wounded breath, 'Help me! Someone help me!" But did I stop? No, I kept running. In fact, I ran faster fearing that I too would face a similar fate unless I put as much distance between myself and the bullets raining on us, put as much distance between that dying body and me, that body whose voice called out and which I ignored."

There was such silence in the room it seemed the world itself was at attention, no axial spinning, just the stillness of injustice gripping it and commanding focus. This man was reaching for the comfort on which many of us rested and like it was a pillow, tearing it into pieces. There could be no indifference to such heavy words. So where was I? I could feel something close to anger building. And also something close to helplessness. I was annoyed at the latter. Remember William Redford. Remember Yannis.

"As it turned out, sixty-eight people, including children, died and a hundred and eighty were wounded. Today, it seems to me that there are at least sixty-eight voices calling to me, to all of us. *Help me. Someone, help me.* Friends, this is a heavy burden that has been placed on us. We are being asked to reach out to those falling under the vicious system of apartheid. The ghosts of that young man and many more like him are asking... We are being asked to take action. Are we going to keep running like I did? Are we going to run away from the problem while others suffer such injustice, denied the pursuit of life and liberty and the pursuit of happiness? That day in Sharpeville, I made a choice and that choice has haunted me since. So what will we do, my brothers and sisters?"

He paused and looked into the audience. It seemed as though he was looking directly at me and I had the impression I wasn't the only one who felt singled out by him in this call. I was ready to sigh with relief that his speech was over. How much more could I take? I remembered Uncle Kusi and his words about the blood shed for independence. I remembered the history lessons of primary school and the bloodletting that occurred as my ancestors defended their land against colonial domination. But Sithole wasn't finished yet.

"About nine days later another march took place in Cape Town, led by a young twenty-three-year old man called Philip Kgosana. Kgosana, fearing bloodshed as in Sharpeville, he dispersed his group before things got out of hand. However, he was arrested later in the evening. The apartheid system was closing in tightly. The ANC was banned on April 6. Forced to operate in the under-waters of such a siege a military wing emerged – the Umkonto we Sizwe, meaning spear of the nations. I was a part of that group, fighting for human dignity, for the right to basic rights. This was, of course, a war of sorts. But the government infiltrated our ranks and started arresting us. At that time, I felt I had no choice but to leave the country. It was this government crackdown that would lead to the arrest of South Africa's famous son, Nelson Mandela. So here I am, a South African, born in Sophiatown, Johannesburg, forced to flee his native land because of the oppressive regime of a government bent on entrenching white minority rule over a black majority. Ladies and gentlemen, this is what we are up against. This is what we must fight and defeat. Any questions?"

A large part of the audience stood to ovate. The first question came from a pale-skinned man, his hair worn long and straight, whose voice seemed to shake (though I couldn't tell if from anger or nervousness). "You paint a grim picture of life in South Africa. What can we do about it, those of us in America?" It was a question I would have liked to ask and I'm sure most of us in the room were thankful that he did.

"I'm glad you raised that question. As you know, the United States government wields enormous influence worldwide. The US government has enormous power to effect change in South Africa. How? The US could impose economic sanctions on South Africa. That would be a start, even if that alone doesn't do the job. The US and other Western countries must isolate the South African government... culturally render it a pariah. But we shouldn't leave it to the government alone. A lot of the pressure can come from the many multinational institutions that have operations in South Africa. As you know, a lot of institutions, including American universities, have investments in companies that operate in South Africa. We must encourage such institutions to divest their interests in such companies, pressure the companies to pull out of South Africa. Write, demonstrate, petition, rally. But please do so peaceably and within the boundaries of rules and laws."

The second question came from a black man I'd not seen before. "What do you say to all those African countries that after independence have resorted to dictatorships, face economic woes and so on? Some say the end of apartheid would lead South Africa down that path. Your response?"

Sithole showed no emotion, his face apparently trained for all manner of questions. "Well, I'm not sure that I have enough time to do due justice to that question, but let me attempt to respond with as much brevity as I can. I must preface this, of course, with the acceptance that a lot of African leaders have abysmally failed to fulfill their promise, the promise of African self-determination. They have sullied their hands with corruption, handicapped by their own avarice and dictatorial tendencies. But you must put it in this context. And I say this not as an excuse or apology, but as just plain fact. Many African countries crumbled to superior technology in the grab for their lands by European powers that were bent on exploiting Africa's resources and adding to their prestige. This grab for African land culminated in the Conference of Berlin in the latter part of the nineteenth century when the European powers decided to partition the continent among themselves. Of course Africa did not have a say in this division of the continent by Europeans. And countries were arbitrarily created without regard to history, ethnicity or local expectations. Apart from the internal tensions this was bound to create and the potential for chaos, it also introduced Africa into the western capitalist markets as exporters of agricultural products in a system so asymmetrical it hurts to think about it. The European powers made sure that African labour would serve to produce raw materials to be bought cheaply by Western industries. So you have small countries, some of them not big enough to support an industrial base, growing and exporting raw materials cheaply for Western markets; you have these weak countries then importing manufactured goods at high prices in exchange; and you have all the internal tensions that come along with countries forced into existence at the whim of European powers. The wide fluctuations in this marketplace handicap the countries of Africa. Not to mention the pillaging of the local resources by these powers. Put all these together and you have enormous odds. African countries are swimming against a mighty tide: corruption of their leaders, an external economic system that is brutally exploitative and a history that has pillaged the continent psychologically and economically. Think about it, my friend. There's my brief summary."

Seventeen

Something changed after Sithole's speech. In it was the clear summons: something had to be done about the situation. It disturbed me, no question. I would ponder over the issues he raised for a long time, feeling helpless, though, to influence anything. I was powerless, I concluded and in all likelihood that is where things would have rested: my return to the usual inertia of the timid, lazy or apathetic. After all, I had a lot on my mind then: law school, Fiona, Ama. But there must have been something larger than me at work, for I was not the only person it had moved – needless to say. So was Dwayne and so was Ed. It was as though a common bolt had passed through us, spreading similar currents. Call it conscience, call it guilt – Sithole had planted a powerful, albeit indirect, directive that mandated action.

And the first person to raise the matter was Dwayne. "Man, I heard the brother. We've got to do something about South Africa. I knew it was bad, brother, but I never really thought about it. You know how it is – you hear about things going on, but they sound so . . . well so distant. And then to know that The Law School is actually contributing to it, that we have investments in South Africa, brother, that just kills me."

"I know, Dwayne," I said. "But the most painful thing is that there's not a thing we can do about it."

"But you're wrong, my brother."

"Oh?"

"I've been thinking, Jojo. I've been thinking. There's something we can do about it. It may not be much, but it will be something. We've got to start somewhere, right?"

"Yes? And what would that be?"

"Protest, my brother. Protest. Remember what Sithole said? What if we begin a protest movement here at The Law School? What if we can get The Law School to divest its financial holdings in South Africa? Won't that be a start? As you and I know, The Law School is a leader in US academia. In fact, come to think of it, it's a leader in the world. If we can get it to divest, who knows which other institutions will follow?"

"Yes, Dwayne, but how can we get The Law School to do that? You think a protest will do it?"

"You never know until you try. Like I said, we have to start somewhere."

"I'm not sure about this, Dwayne."

"Think about it."

I did think about it. I was worried that a protest would simply be wooing danger. I wanted my law degree badly as a step towards financial security and was afraid of doing anything to put that prospect in jeopardy. In casual conversation, I mentioned the idea of a protest to Ed, "Sounds like a great thing," he said. "Hey, I'd be more than willing to protest on this issue." I told that to Dwayne. "If even a white boy is willing to do this, how can we not?" He had an undeniable point there. Could I continue to live in the selfish shell of self-advancement? Could I continue to justify my own existence without a linkage to some higher calling, whatever it might be? I didn't have to wallow in this existentialist uncertainty for long. A week later Dwayne was organising the protest. It was to be a midday rally, scheduled for the following Wednesday. Dwayne organised it under the auspices of the Black Law Students Association, but he sent invitations to a broad range of students and student organizations. The invitation notice had the BLSA's logo inconspicuously in small print at its bottom. The event was simply billed as a protest against the inhumane apartheid system. It made no mention of divestiture. It made no mention of The Law School. Not many could resist such a call – a call to protest an injustice that must have pricked the conscience of modern America, or a portion of it.

Ed and I went to the rally together. I noticed that John was there as well. "I didn't expect you here, John," I said. "I had no idea this would interest you."

"Well, to be honest with you, Jojo, I'm here on assignment for *The Law Record*." I noticed he held a pad and pen.

"Well, this time you better get your facts right," I said.

"Come on, give me some professional integrity."

The protest was underway in no time. It was difficult to determine an exact count. My guess was that there were about three hundred students present – about a third of the student population. Not bad at all. Dwayne began with a short speech: "We're here today to mourn and protest something that eats like a cancer on the soul of all of us." *Cancer on our soul*. Is that something from your father's poems, I wanted to ask, but didn't. "Apartheid is the cancer," he added. "I could go on and on about how evil this system is, but if you are here today, you probably know it already. So the question becomes how we, living in the US, can help change the system. We're not asking that anybody take up arms and go fighting. All we're asking is that you join us to protest our own institution's support for the system. I was appalled to find out that The Law School has investments in many corporations that do business in South Africa. Today we send a message loud and clear to The Law School: No more. No more financial support for a system that treats its coloured citizens as second-class citizens or worse. No more financial support for a brutal regime that wantonly destroys the lives of its citizenry…" Three others followed him, it seemed carefully selected for their ability to speak as much as their racial makeup: Caucasian, Asian and Native American. I had declined the invitation to speak.

We followed the speeches with a march, Dwayne, Ed and I and a part of the crowd. It was a relatively vociferous, multiracial group that started the march with the song "*We Shall Overcome*". Then it became vocal in its chanting, varied from time to time as we marched through campus:

WE WANT JUSTICE!

WHEN DO WE WANT IT?

NOW!

DIVEST! DIVEST! DIVEST FROM
SOUTH AFRICA NOW!
APARTHEID MUST END!

WHEN MUST IT END?
NOW!

And the most popular chant:

FREE NELSON MANDELA!

Various members of the group carried placards bearing similar messages. Marching within the group, I was possessed by power I didn't consider possible until then. It was as though I was absorbing every ounce of energy around me as much as I was giving. This give and take – call it spiritual symbiosis – fortified me beyond description, empowering me, strengthening my belief in the cause and in its success. This cause was morally right and had to have an audience. In all, the march spanned about two hours, by which time it was evening and we were mostly hoarse. We converged again at the starting point. Dwayne thanked all the demonstrators and dispersed the group with the exhortation: "We shall keep protesting until The Law School heeds our call. Keep up the spirit with your eyes on the prize." Ed and I were dispersing with the rest, our duty to the cause done (at least for the moment), when Dwayne hurried to us. "You know what?" he said. "I prepared a formal petition to the Dean. I want to make this more low key for now. Just us. How about you come with me to the Dean's office?"

It was an offer we couldn't reject: the rightness of the cause so strongly pontificated; the strength of the march still extant and the request from Dwayne so honouring. "Sure," I said.

"And you, Ed?"

"Me?" said Ed. "Yeah, why not?"

It would have been this group of three, but John was hovering around us, his pen and pad in hand. He'd overhead. "I'm coming too," he said. "Boy is this getting more interesting than I imagined?"

"You're not following us in there with that pad and paper," said Dwayne.

"Come on. This is the perfect press you need."

Dwayne hesitated a moment. "Okay," he said. "But you have to put the pen and paper away. I don't want him thinking we are orchestrating this just for the press."

So grouped, we marched to the Dean's office. His secretary told us to wait after Dwayne insisted we had to see the Dean immediately. She left for a brief while. "I'll be happy to schedule an appointment for you sometime during the week,' she said upon returning. "The Dean is tied up right now."

"This will only take a minute," Dwayne said. "We have to see him right away."

"I'm sorry, sir. He can't see you right now."

"He can't or he won't?"

"Look, sir…"

Dwayne hurried past her, going in the direction of the Dean's office. The rest of us felt compelled to follow him. Dwayne opened the door to the office and rushed in. The Dean jumped from his desk, clearly baffled. "What are you doing? Didn't they tell you I couldn't see anyone at this time?"

"Sir, this is just a petition we want to give to you."

"I'm going to have to ask you to leave," said the Dean. "Schedule an appointment and I will receive your petition."

Dwayne took the written petition from his pocket and walked closer to the Dean, holding the petition out.

"Don't come closer!" yelled the Dean. "Leave! Now!"

"Sir, all I'm asking is that you take this petition and we'll be out of here."

"You have to do this the right way. I'm not touching that paper until you schedule an appointment and do this the right way."

"The right way? Sir, just take it."

The Dean was visibly livid. His brow furrowed, his eyes glared, his cheeks flushed red, his nostrils flared and his lips twitched. I too was infuriated at the arrogance (or I deemed it so) with which he dismissed Dwayne and by extension, all of us. He moved forward towards us, saying, "Are you leaving or do you want me to call security?"

"Security?" asked Dwayne. "What for?"

"Okay," he said. "That's it." He reached for the phone.

It was as if an extraordinarily bizarre force had seized me – was this some sort of out-of-body experience? – as I rushed forward, put my hand over the Dean's and prevented him from lifting the receiver to his ear. He was beyond shock and exasperation as his lips opened and for seconds he struggled fruitlessly to speak. He lifted his other arm and started waiving his finger at me. "I'm warning you," finally came the voice from his reddened face. He said it with such authority that the invading force within me seemed irked even more. That occupying *energy* seemed to raise my hand. I wanted to tell it to calm down but it moved faster than my thoughts. My hand came down heavily across the Dean's face.

"My God!" The Dean yelped. If the silence that descended upon the room could be seen with naked eyes, it would be denser than mist.

By then, five security guards and the Dean's secretary were already in the room (the Dean's secretary having taken the initiative to summon them). The Dean started to say he wanted the campus police called immediately to his office, but then he changed his mind and had Security check our student IDs for our names instead. "Please escort these gentlemen from my office," he asked the security guards. And so ended (or rather, began?) the episode of the *Group of Four's* assault on the Dean of The Law School.

We were all so solemn after we were led out. And for minutes no one had the courage to speak. This extension of our actions, which had been so unplanned and unexpected, was steering us in an as yet indecipherable direction. I personally felt as much of that group as I felt detached from it. And gone was the power I had experienced so recently when I marched as part of the crowd. Now, the heaviness of what I'd done visited me without the guise of that power: I had assaulted the Dean of The Law School. That was the fact. What would be the consequence? I couldn't determine yet, but I knew there would be retribution. There had to be, but the Administration teased us for a long time with silence.

A week later, the Administration ended its silence with a terse note in each of our mailboxes: *Report to the Assistant Dean's office at 3pm on Wednesday for consideration of matters involving recent activities connected with your assault on the Dean.* I was extremely worried. Dwayne and Ed both tried to cheer me, but I knew they too were concerned. John was silent for the most part but, after all, he could argue that he wasn't really part of us. So far he hadn't, which I found surprising.

The Assistant Dean sat solo behind his huge desk when we marched *en masse* into his office. He had prepared for us, it seemed, as four chairs were arranged in front of his desk. He puffed on his pipe without asking if the smoke bothered us. Almost dwarfing his desk, he pulled on his nose. *Mr. Redford, where art thou?* "Gentlemen," he said. A forced cough confirmed to me that he was nervous, which I found rather odd in that I thought we were the ones under probe, subject to administrative discipline, or whatever they might call it. But what he would say next drew me to a better understanding. Here he was, a representative of the Administration and he too was constrained. "The Dean asked me to summon you here to arrange the terms of what we intend to do with your... your case. A number of people have expressed the view that he ought to press charges for assault. But he has no present intention of doing that."

Very clever words: *No present intention*; not *he won't*. I took note.

"I must say he is rather perplexed by what happened the other day, that matters would become so explosive. But the Dean wants fairness here. He wants to give you an opportunity for a hearing before the Disciplinary Board. Of course, you will be entitled to have a member of the faculty represent you. But as you can understand, this can be quite... shall I say, explosive. Therefore, it is necessary, imperative that you not do anything to add fuel to the situation. I hope that is clear."

He wasn't expecting a response.

"Any questions, gentlemen?"

We had none.

"Very well then, the hearing is scheduled a week from today. You soon shall receive details in your mailbox.

Meanwhile, I'd suggest that you think about which faculty member you'd want to represent you . . . if you so choose. The sooner the better, of course . . . to give him time to prepare your defense."

What gave me hope was the implicit bargain. We were being asked not to take any further action in pursuit of divestiture – no rallies or protests – in return for which the Dean would not press his case and for which (who knows) we might get some leniency from the Disciplinary Board. After the meeting with the Assistant Dean, John urged that we get ourselves a lawyer. "We will have one from the faculty," I said. "They are all lawyers."

"No way," countered John. "There's a clear conflict right there. How can we expect them to be impartial?"

I feared that seeking to raise the bar would defeat the compromise the Administration was offering. In my view, they were concerned that this might get out of their control, that it could become a political matter that would sully the name of the school. They wanted our cooperation in keeping it low key. To bring an outside lawyer into the carefully calibrated equation would remove all bets from the table. I couldn't have that happen. In the end, we decided with a vote, which I won three to one. Having decided to pick someone from the faculty, we had to decide whom. Unanimously, we agreed on Professor Janet O'Grady. She'd taught me Civil Procedure. I liked her.

Eighteen

Professor Janet O'Grady agreed to defend us. She and *The Group of Four* sat on one side of the room. On the other side were the assistant dean (to serve as the arbitrator of the proceedings) and Professor Lewis Jenkins, professor of criminal law (to present The Law School's case). Did they have to pick someone conversant with criminal law? In the middle were members of the Disciplinary Board (to act as the jury), comprising three students (none of whom I knew) and six members of the faculty (none of whom I knew either). If this was a juror of my peers, what hope did I have in the whiteness that confronted me? The only people of colour in this constituent body were Janet O'Grady, Dwayne and I. We were all seated on one side and the rest seemed to be separated from us.

The assistant dean called the proceedings to order in a calm, seemingly calculated tone of voice that sounded more threatening than if he'd have yelled. His power seemed on a par with Sithole's. His invitation to Professor Larry Jenkins to present the case followed a pause that appeared inserted to cause tension, create suspense as in a striptease. Larry Jenkins rose large in front of us, tall, debonair, lithe, hair all grey. The paced voice matched well the dignity of form. He had no notes as he stood behind the desk to present his case. "This matter is straightforward and warrants no prolonged introduction," he said. "The facts are not in dispute. On a Wednesday two weeks ago, these students: John Owens, Dwayne Dray, Edward Palmer, and Jojo Badu, with *intent* to assault him, walked to the dean's office and demanded to see the dean. The dean's secretary asked them, like all other students, to schedule an appointment. They refused. Instead, they barged into his office and demanded that he accept a petition. When he asked them to be patient and wait for an appointment, one of them, Jojo Badu, assaulted and battered the dean, slapping him across the face. These are the bare facts . . . "

Bare facts, Mr Jenkins? Intent to assault the dean? Assault and Battery?

Professor O'Grady went next. "The facts are straightforward enough, but not in the way Professor Jenkins presents them. Yes, these students did go to the dean's office. But they asked, they didn't *demand,* to see the dean. Knowing that the dean had no appointment then and having been refused access to the dean as they are entitled to, the students walked into the dean's office. They asked if the dean would consider their petition. Now, I'm sure the dean had his reasons for protocol, but as much as we don't attribute bad intentions to the dean, we shouldn't attribute any to the students. It was only after the dean said he would call security, it was only after the students feared imminent harm, afraid of the consequences, attempting to stop the dean from calling security, that one of them accidentally hit the dean."

Which version of the facts would be believed? Was it even necessary what I thought? From the very beginning, the charade was clear and we had to play the part. Where would we find objectivity when the Disciplinary Board was so heavily skewed in favour of the Faculty? Was the result not a foregone conclusion? Wouldn't we all save time by packing pen and paper and resting limb and breath by walking away? But no, the *system* had to be served, its fetishes appeased with the sacrifices of simulated fair play, the belief in the justness of its accoutrements affirmed in this theatrical performance, all of us under the unseen puppeteer's control, the strings jerking us in its well orchestrated performance. Neither the dean nor any one of us had much control, unless we severed the strings, but would that not fling us out of the stage on which we all wanted to participate? Were we all not afraid (or had we not chosen) that being controlled onstage was preferable to freedom offstage and living with the delusion that we had our freedoms or that we could change the plot onstage? Oh, what contradictions.

Larry Jenkins was now questioning his first witness: the dean's secretary, Anita James. She parroted his version of events. And now it was Janet O'Grady's turn to examine her. "Ms James, you've given us a very interesting version of what transpired that evening, but there's more to it than that, isn't there? I ask you this, did Mr Dray yell at you when he requested to see the dean?"

"No."

"Did any of the other students?"

"No."

"In fact, that was not the first time you'd seen Mr Dray, was it?"

"No."

"When had you last seen him?"

"He had come to see me the day before."

"And what did he ask when he came to see you?"

"He wanted to set up an appointment."

"To see the dean?"

"Yes."

"And what did you tell him?"

"He wanted to see the dean the next day, he said, but he wasn't sure what time he would be there. He said he had to see the dean after a rally the next day, but not knowing exactly when the rally would end, he asked whether he could stop by in the evening."

"And what did you tell him?"

"I said he could."

"And did you talk to the dean about Mr Dray's visit?"

Anita James seemed surprised by that question. She looked to Larry Jenkins as if seeking help. Jenkins quickly interposed: "This line of questioning isn't necessary. It really adds nothing to the deliberations here."

The assistant dean concurred: "Professor Grady, I would suggest that you avoid this line of questioning."

Professor O'Grady had no choice. She too was engaged in the play and she could not force the plot to deviate too much if she were to continue as a part of it. I was even afraid she'd stretched it too far, for the implication was clear: Anita Jenkins must have talked to the dean about Dwayne's wish to present a petition and the dean must have asked that she not allow him in at all or not allow him in without an appointment. That would be the most benign reading of Professor O'Grady's question. She desisted from pursuing further that route of enquiry.

Then Larry Jenkins called the head security guard, whose main testimony was that Anita James had called her, worried about a group of students who'd barged into the dean's office. She was concerned for the dean's safety after she heard yelling in his office. "Did she say who was doing the yelling?" Professor O'Grady asked.

"No, she didn't."

"It could have been the dean then?"

"I had the impression it wasn't the dean."

"Impression. Did you know for a fact?"

"No, ma'am."

"When you entered the room, did you see any of the students attacking the dean?"

"No, ma'am."

"Did you see any of them yelling at him?"

"No, ma'am."

The prosecution rested.

The defense started with Professor O'Grady asking Dwayne what happened. He reiterated his intention to present his petition to the dean. The petition was to ask The Law School to consider divesting from South Africa. He had planned to do it alone all along, but he thought it would have more legitimacy if he had some numbers, so at the very last minute, he'd asked Ed, John and I to join him. Why hadn't he just sent it by mail? He thought it would be more effective if he did it in person: "You know, put a face to the words."

Larry Jenkins tried to create the impression that there'd been some sort of conspiracy all along. "Are you not friends with the other students?"

"Yes, I am."

Really, Dwayne? Even John?

"And you'd seen them before the day of the rally, hadn't you?"

"Not really. The only one I'd seen with some regularity was Jojo. And honestly, I don't remember the last time I'd seen John."

One by one, we were asked to testify. Ed went after Dwayne, confirming the latter's version of events. John's went similarly. And then it was my turn. I too made a brief confirmation of the others' story. Professor O'Grady avoided the one question that everyone in the room must have been asking: *Why did you hit the Dean*? Instead, she asked a series of questions designed to take me step by step from the point when I had entered the room, seen the dean reject Dwayne's offer to receive the petition and then, "So you saw the dean lift the phone?"

"Yes."

"And what did you do?"

"I panicked that he was going to call security and make it appear that we were posing some form of security threat. I moved forward to try and convince him not to call anyone, to just take the petition and we would be on our way, but things seemed to happen so fast and next thing I knew, I accidentally brushed my hand against his face."

Come now Jojo, which idiot will believe this cock and bull story?

Professor Jenkins wasn't satisfied with that, but he was boxed in just as we all were: to argue too forcefully for a premeditated assault would mandate a harsh punishment, which it seemed they wanted to avoid in order not to inflame the situation. So, against the risk that I could come up with a sympathetic answer and as if reluctantly, he asked the taboo question: "Mr. Badu, why did you strike the dean?"

I answered. He asked that I say it again. "Mr. Badu, we need to hear what you're saying. Would you speak a little louder?"

I did, repeating what I'd said a little louder. "I didn't mean to touch him, sir. It was an accident."

But, sir, could I tell you the real reason(s)? Did I know all the reasons? And if I did, would I be able to sum it up in those stale minutes? If I could, I would have told him it would take a voluminous manuscript to answer that question. Sir, if you really want to know, find that manuscript. And read it fairly without prejudice. Perhaps then and only then, would you be in a situation to offer fair play and substantial justice.

Three days later, we each received a note, which read in relevant part:

> The Disciplinary Committee of the Law School has decided formally to warn you to desist from any future provocative actions. The Committee has decided to place you on probation. Any such actions in the future may result in stricter disciplinary action, including dismissal from The Law School.

We had been punished, but not as severely as I'd feared. Or perhaps it was an offer of friendship of sorts? But with our hands so deeply intertwined with one another, we had none to extend to the administration even if we wanted to do so. It was a victory and John invited us to his apartment for a celebration. It was just the four of us, no administration hanging over our heads and the threat of what they might do to affect our futures, no students supporting or judging and no disconnections between us at that time. We had momentarily eased the tension that had besieged us before. We had fought and lost and won.

We were united and the victory was the glue for the gathering. Even Dwayne didn't hesitate to accept the invitation. With John's unicorn staring, we shared champagne (supplied by John) and good laughs. It would have stayed without substantive discussion had not Ed toasted Professor O'Grady and then mentioned her upcoming consideration for tenure. "I hope she gets it. It will be a damn shame if they deny her tenure. She's such a great person."

"Well, that may be her problem," Dwayne said. "She's got too much of the earth instinct."

"Earth instinct?" I asked. "What's that?"

Dwayne hesitated as if he didn't want to soil our giddiness with the heavy statement he was about to make, somewhat incongruous considering the occasion. I asked him again to explain it. "It's a term derived from the difference between black and white... the kinds of people we are. I have come up with this theory about the nature of blacks and whites. You see, white people, they've got the mechanical instinct. What's the mechanical instinct? It's the instinct within them that strives to explore, to be adventurous. The mechanical instinct sees a mountain and wants to climb it and get to the top of it just because it's there. It is the instinct that wants to explore the moon and conquer it. It's the instinct that doesn't rest until it has bettered what another has or taken it away and made it its own. That instinct isn't bound to the earth. It is bound to what can be made out of the earth; therefore, it builds machines and arsenals. That is the mechanical instinct."

"And the earth instinct?" Ed asked.

"The earth instinct... that is the instinct of black people. They are bound to the earth and not what is processed out of it. It is the instinct that enjoys moments under the tree shade, the warmth of the sun. It is the instinct that holds a brother's or sister's hands and then another's and is satisfied to hold those hands. It is the instinct that does not seek to explore the mystery on the horizon, but to explain it as the work of God. Therefore, it doesn't bother with relationships with machines, but with relationships with others of the earth. That is the earth instinct."

"You are full of crap," said Ed.

"No, I'm not. Look, it is the reason why white folks went exploring other continents and conquering other lands where they had no business."

"So which is the better instinct?" I asked.

"That depends. You see, with the mechanical instinct, you may make great strides in science and that kind of stuff. So in a way, the mechanical instinct improves our quality of life. But it also leads to mass pollution, the building of bombs capable of annihilating the human race. It reduces the importance of human relationships, our interconnectedness with one another and puts it at a mechanical, awful, level where everything is forced, perfunctory. The earth instinct doesn't build those machines, but it creates warmth between people, an inner happiness, solidarity. I don't know if these instincts shift from people to people or race to race during the course of history. But the fact of the matter is, when the mechanical and earth instincts meet, the mechanical instinct dominates, for better or for worse. Think of steel plunging into the earth. That's the way it is."

"On what basis do you draw these conclusions?" asked John.

"My own observation, although it is not an entirely original idea. And let me add a little footnote. It is a generalization, of course. Some combine both instincts in varying degrees, between and among races."

"I can't believe you're saying this," John said. "Wouldn't you call me a racist if I said what you're saying?"

"I don't know. Perhaps I would."

"But that's applying a double standard."

"Yep. But that's America for you."

"You know," I said, "This theory of instincts sounds very much to me like Negritude. I remember Leopold Senghor's famous statement 'Emotion is black as Reason is Hellenic,' which has been severely criticised in some circles."

"Whatever!" John exclaimed. "Let's drink to the earth instinct. Let's drink to the mechanical instinct." We complied. I was even giddier when I left his apartment.

Nineteen

I reflected later. I'd attempted to take a bold stance, unlike the way I'd been dragged into it at The University. But I'd been neutralised. I vowed I wouldn't follow that path again, steering clear of politics when I remembered how it had pulled Uncle Kusi to his death even when he only stood in its fringes. I would focus more on my career as a law student. Moreover, although not directly impacting me, I was increasingly disillusioned about politics by the brewing Watergate scandal. I watched as G. Gordon Liddy and James McCord were convicted and Attorney General Richard Kleindeinst resigned; I read about the firing of the special prosecutor Archibald Cox, the resignation of Spiro Agnew over charges of racketeering and tax evasion, the voting of articles of impeachment against President Nixon for interfering in the Watergate investigation and his eventual resignation. A bad shadow seemed overcast on American politics. I had had my own taste on a smaller scale. They combined to make me foreswear all things political. So the next year of law school I spent studying and keeping with family and friends. The work was more familiar and not as stressful. I never volunteered in class and was hardly called on. Perhaps the name Jojo Badu wasn't appealing to my professors. With a half-hearted effort I wrote my third year dissertation on the redundancy of grand juries – *what a witty topic, Jojo*. I got a B for it. Fiona and Ama and I took long strolls in the park, becoming better friends. I spoke with Fiona about the challenges of law school. She listened intently. I must have conveyed something positive to her, for it was during my last year of law school that she decided it was time for her to go to law school. No! I wanted to tell her. Law School had been hard, dreary and weary. How, though, could I dissuade her from a path I'd picked for myself? She applied and as she'd done for me, I encouraged and supported her.

Fiona had gotten pregnant again. Juju was born a few months before Fiona started law school. The Law School turned her down, but she got into Boston University. This time Fiona was adamant that I stay with her in the delivery room. It was together or not at all, she insisted. I didn't understand what she meant by "or not at all." I took no chances. I held on to her as she was encouraged to push. She screamed and made noises I didn't know existed in vocal chords. But the beauty of a baby coming from its mother . . . so helpless and vulnerable, so beautiful. I was enthralled, overcome by a sense of insignificance in this magic of birth, creation in its most fundamental testimony to itself. Tears swelled up in my eyes when I saw the baby for the first time and my heartbeat welled with joy and pride and love when I heard the baby cry. (Oh, and how I wished I'd been there for Ama's birth as well.) The year was 1974. I had two children.

Professor Janet O'Grady was denied tenure at The Law School. Had she gone too far defending us? She was offered employment at another less prestigious law school. Fiona became a law student that fall. It made things more complicated as we had to take care of two children – one about five years and the other only months old. I'd never seen a more determined woman than Fiona. It seemed she'd suddenly acquired a new gusto, breastfeeding Jojo for a brief period (ending it sooner than I'd have liked), playing with Ama, studying and still remaining sane. She had it, more than I.

In the final year of law school, I applied for jobs with several law firms. After a drill of sixty and three interviews, I received one offer. Not that the dreariness of interviewing was that unique to me. We all had to endure the process of reading about the law firm ahead of time to gain some knowledge peculiar to it – its partners, reputation, history or demographics – that set it apart, that we could use to impress interviewers; working through the resume to make sure it had no errors and contained only that which would impress the interviewer and then making sure every notation on it was defensible; the spending of my paltry financial aid on a suit (the second one I'd ever owned), a tie, decent shoes, all of which had to be relatively conservative in order to conform with the expectation of law firms; the scheduling of interviews around or even during classes; and then the interview itself. But in my case was the added surprise, it seemed, when I walked into the room and spoke with an accent to which the interviewers weren't accustomed. I remember one interview in particular when I had to sit through request upon request to repeat what I'd just said. I recalled interviewers who asked me to repeat my name several times and still mispronounced it, or pulled faces when I said it. I remembered interviewers who asked me why I didn't want to go back to my *country*; interviewers who lost interest in me the minute I walked into the room. But I endured it all because I was desperate for a job. And after all that, to receive only one offer... What such near unanimous rejection does to a man's ego needs no repeating. I'd watched friends with anywhere from five to fifteen job offers struggling to make a choice. Sure, I was spared the *agony* of that choice, just dealt the emasculating blow of self-doubt.

Preparing for the bar exam after graduation took much cramming in a short period of time, most of it on subject matters I'd not studied in law school and would never encounter again. I took and passed the Massachusetts bar exam and looked forward to working fulltime for the mid-sized law firm Preston, Ingold, Thomas & Slaughter. Dwayne headed for a mid-sized law firm in DC and Ed a major one in Boston. John had graduated the year before and joined a law firm in DC, intimating to me before he left that he intended to run for national office some day. Given our past, I was convinced that my path would continue to intersect with theirs one way or another.

I looked back in time as I embraced my new job, considering myself a continuing sojourner, who had triumphed over pitfalls and would face more in the foreseeable future. I was not sure I could adequately answer the question presented: whether the day of my arrival in the US was to be blessed or cursed. But, with two children and a loving wife, I was convinced my future in America held much promise. The only pertinent question left at the time was whether I could fulfill that promise. And as I considered how far I had journeyed, something like an unshakable resolve lodged inside me and I said to myself: *All is renewed and my life starts again.*

* * *